NATHANAEL WEST was born in New York City in 1903 and died on the West Coast in an automobile accident in 1940. During his short life he completed four novels, of which MISS LONELYHEARTS in the opinion of critic Stanley Edgar Hyman, is the one most clearly assured of permanent survival.

He graduated in 1924 from Brown University, after which he spent two happy years in Paris, returning to New York and a variety of odd jobs. THE DREAM LIFE OF BALSO SNELL was privately published in a limited edition of 500 copies in 1931 and attracted little attention at the time, although its reputation is gaining with the rise of the modern picaresque novel; in 1933, however, his classic MISS LONELYHEARTS was enthusiastically received. West's last years were spent in California as a film script writer, but during the period he published two other short works, A COOL MILLION and his famous Hollywood novel, THE DAY OF THE LOCUST.

THE DREAM LIFE OF BALSO SNELL and A COOL MILLION are also available in one volume, in an Avon Library edition.

MISS LONELYHEARTS

Nathanael West

With an afterword by
STANLEY EDGAR HYMAN

An Avon Library Book

AVON BOOKS
A division of
The Hearst Corporation
959 Eighth Avenue
New York, New York 10019

First Avon Printing, March, 1955
Fourth Avon Printing, November, 1962
First Avon Library Edition (Fifth Printing), February, 1964
Third Avon Library Edition (Seventh Printing), June, 1967

Cover design by Nick Fasciano

Miss Lonelyhearts

Help Me, Help Me

THE MISS LONELYHEARTS of The New York *Post-Dispatch* (Are-you-in-trouble? — Do-you-need-advice? — Write-to-Miss-Lonelyhearts-and-she-will-help-you) sat at his desk and stared at a piece of white cardboard. On it a prayer had been printed by Shrike, the feature editor.

> "*Soul of Miss L, glorify me.*
> *Body of Miss L, nourish me.*
> *Blood of Miss L, intoxicate me.*
> *Tears of Miss L, wash me.*
> *Oh good Miss L, excuse my plea,*
> *And hide me in your heart,*
> *And defend me from mine enemies.*
> *Help me, Miss L, help me, help me.*
> *In sæcula sæculorum. Amen.*"

Although the deadline was less than a quarter of an hour away, he was still working on his leader. He had gone as far as: "Life *is* worth while, for it is full of dreams and peace, gentleness and ecstasy, and faith that burns like a clear white flame on a grim dark altar." But he found it impossible to continue. The letters were no longer funny. He could not go on finding the same joke funny thirty times a day for months on end. And on most days he received more than thirty letters, all of them alike, stamped from the dough of suffering with a heart-shaped cookie knife.

On his desk were piled those he had received this morning. He started through them again, searching for some clue to a sincere answer.

Dear Miss Lonelyhearts—

I am in such pain I dont know what to do sometimes I think I will kill myself my kidneys hurt so much. My husband thinks no woman can be a good catholic and not have children irregardless of the pain. I was married honorable from our church but I never knew what married life meant as I never was told about man and wife. My grandmother never told me and she was the only mother I had but made a big mistake by not telling me as it dont pay to be inocent and is only a big disapointment. I have 7 children in 12 yrs and ever since the last 2 I have been so sick. I was operated on twice and my husband promised no more children on the doctors advice as he said I might die but when I

got back from the hospital he broke his promise and now I am going to have a baby and I
don't think I can stand it my kidneys hurt so
much. I am so sick and scared because I cant
have an abortion on account of being a catholic and my husband so religious. I cry all the
time it hurts so much and I don't know what
to do.

Yours respectfully,
Sick-of-it-all

Miss Lonelyhearts threw the letter into an open
drawer and lit a cigarette.

Dear Miss Lonelyhearts—

I am sixteen years old now and I dont
know what to do and would appreciate it if
you could tell me what to do. When I was a
little girl it was not so bad because I got used
to the kids on the block makeing fun of me,
but now I would like to have boy friends like
other girls and go out on Saturday nites, but
no boy will take me because I was born without a nose—although I am a good dancer and
have a nice shape and my father buys me
pretty clothes.

I sit and look at myself all day and cry. I
have a big hole in the middle of my face that
scares people even myself so I cant blame
the boys for not wanting to take me out. My
mother loves me, but she crys terrible when
she looks at me.

What did I do to deserve such a terrible

*bad fate? Even if I did do some bad things I
didn't do any before I was a year old and I
was born this way. I asked Papa and he says
he doesnt know, but that maybe I did something in the other world before I was born or
that maybe I was being punished for his sins.
I dont believe that because he is a very nice
man. Ought I commit suicide?*

Sincerely yours,
Desperate

The cigarette was imperfect and refused to draw.
Miss Lonelyhearts took it out of his mouth and
stared at it furiously. He fought himself quiet, then
lit another one.

Dear Miss Lonelyhearts—
*I am writing to you for my little sister
Gracie because something awfull hapened to
her and I am afraid to tell mother about it. I
am 15 years old and Gracie is 13 and we live
in Brooklyn. Gracie is deaf and dumb and
biger than me but not very smart on account
of being deaf and dumb. She plays on the
roof of our house and dont go to school except to deaf and dumb school twice a week
on tuesdays and thursdays. Mother makes
her play on the roof because we dont want
her to get run over as she aint very smart.
Last week a man came on the roof and did
something dirty to her. She told me about it
and I dont know what to do as I am afraid to
tell mother on account of her being liable to*

beat Gracie up. I am afraid that Gracie is going to have a baby and I listened to her stomack last night for a long time to see if I could hear the baby but I couldn't. If I tell mother she will beat Gracie up awfull because I am the only one who loves her and last time when she tore her dress they loked her in the closet for 2 days and if the boys on the blok hear about it they will say dirty things like they did on Peewee Conors sister the time she got caught in the lots. So please what could you do if the same hapened in your family.

Yours truly,
Harold S.

He stopped reading. Christ was the answer, but, if he did not want to get sick, he had to stay away from the Christ business. Besides, Christ was Shrike's particular joke. "Soul of Miss L, glorify me. Body of Miss L, save me. Blood of . . ." He turned to his typewriter.

Although his cheap clothes had too much style, he still looked like the son of a Baptist minister. A beard would become him, would accent his Old-Testament look. But even without a beard no one could fail to recognize the New England puritan. His forehead was high and narrow. His nose was long and fleshless. His bony chin was shaped and cleft like a hoof. On seeing him for the first time, Shrike had smiled and said, "The Susan Chesters, the Beatrice Fairfaxes and the Miss Lonelyhearts are the priests of twentieth-century America."

A copy boy came up to tell him that Shrike wanted to know if the stuff was ready. He bent over the typewriter and began pounding its keys.

But before he had written a dozen words, Shrike leaned over his shoulder. "The same old stuff," Shrike said. "Why don't you give them something new and hopeful? Tell them about art. Here, I'll dictate:

"*Art is a Way Out.*

"Do not let life overwhelm you. When the old paths are choked with the débris of failure, look for newer and fresher paths. Art is just such a path. Art is distilled from suffering. As Mr. Polnikoff exclaimed through his fine Russian beard, when, at the age of eighty-six, he gave up his business to learn Chinese, 'We are, as yet, only at the beginning. . . .'

"*Art is One of Life's Richest offerings.*

"For those who have not the talent to create, there is appreciation. For those . . .

"Go on from there."

Miss Lonelyhearts

and the Dead Pan

WHEN MISS LONELYHEARTS quit work, he found that the weather had turned warm and that the air smelt as though it had been artificially heated. He decided to walk to Delehanty's speakeasy for a drink. In order to get there, it was necessary to cross a little park.

He entered the park at the North Gate and swallowed mouthfuls of the heavy shade that curtained its arch. He walked into the shadow of a lamp-post that lay on the path like a spear. It pierced him like a spear.

As far as he could discover, there were no signs of spring. The decay that covered the surface of the mottled ground was not the kind in which life generates. Last year, he remembered, May had failed to quicken these soiled fields. It had taken all the brutality of July to torture a few green spikes through the exhausted dirt.

What the little park needed, even more than he did, was a drink. Neither alcohol nor rain would do. Tomorrow, in his column, he would ask Broken-hearted, Sick-of-it-all, Desperate, Disillusioned-with-tubercular-husband and the rest of his correspondents to come here and water the soil with their tears. Flowers would then spring up, flowers that smelled of feet.

"Ah, humanity . . ." But he was heavy with shadow and the joke went into a dying fall. He tried to break its fall by laughing at himself.

Why laugh at himself, however, when Shrike was waiting at the speakeasy to do a much better job? "Miss Lonelyhearts, my friend, I advise you to give your readers stones. When they ask for bread don't give them crackers as does the Church, and don't, like the State, tell them to eat cake. Explain that man cannot live by bread alone and give them stones. Teach them to pray each morning: 'Give us this day our daily stone.' "

He had given his readers many stones; so many, in fact, that he had only one left—the stone that had formed in his gut.

Suddenly tired, he sat down on a bench. If he could only throw the stone. He searched the sky for a target. But the gray sky looked as if it had been rubbed with a soiled eraser. It held no angels, flaming crosses, olive-bearing doves, wheels within wheels. Only a newspaper struggled in the air like a kite with a broken spine. He got up and started again for the speakeasy.

Delehanty's was in the cellar of a brownstone house that differed from its more respectable neighbors by having an armored door. He pressed a concealed button and a little round window opened in its center. A blood-shot eye appeared, glowing like a ruby in an antique iron ring.

The bar was only half full. Miss Lonelyhearts looked around apprehensively for Shrike and was relieved at not finding him. However, after a third drink, just as he was settling into the warm mud of alcoholic gloom, Shrike caught his arm.

"Ah, my young friend!" he shouted. "How do I find you? Brooding again, I take it."

"For Christ's sake, shut up."

Shrike ignored the interruption. "You're morbid, my friend, morbid. Forget the crucifixion, remember the renaissance. There were no brooders then." He raised his glass, and the whole Borgia family was in his gesture. "I give you the renaissance. What a period! What pageantry! Drunken popes...Beautiful courtesans...Illegitimate children...."

Although his gestures were elaborate, his face was blank. He practiced a trick used much by moving-picture comedians—the dead pan. No matter how fantastic or excited his speech, he never changed his expression. Under the shining white globe of his brow, his features huddled together in a dead, gray triangle.

"To the renaissance!" he kept shouting. "To the renaissance! To the brown Greek manuscripts and mistresses with great smooth marbly limbs.... But that reminds me, I'm expecting one of my admirers —a cow-eyed girl of great intelligence." He illustrated the word *intelligence* by carving two enormous breasts in the air with his hands. "She works in a book store, but wait until you see her behind."

Miss Lonelyhearts made the mistake of showing his annoyance.

"Oh, so you don't care for women, eh? J. C. is your only sweetheart, eh? Jesus Christ, the King of Kings, the Miss Lonelyhearts of Miss Lonelyhearts. . . ."

At this moment, fortunately for Miss Lonelyhearts, the young woman expected by Shrike came up to the bar. She had long legs, thick ankles, big hands, a powerful body, a slender neck and a childish face made tiny by a man's haircut.

"Miss Farkis," Shrike said, making her bow as a ventriloquist does his doll, "Miss Farkis, I want you to meet Miss Lonelyhearts. Show him the same respect you show me. He, too, is a comforter of the poor in spirit and a lover of God."

She acknowledged the introduction with a masculine handshake.

"Miss Farkis," Shrike said, "Miss Farkis works in a book store and writes on the side." He patted her rump.

"What were you talking about so excitedly?" she asked.

"Religion."

"Get me a drink and please continue. I'm very much interested in the new thomistic synthesis."

This was just the kind of remark for which Shrike was waiting. "St. Thomas!" he shouted. "What do you take us for—stinking intellectuals? We're not fake Europeans. We were discussing Christ, the Miss Lonelyhearts of Miss Lonelyhearts. America has her own religions. If you need a synthesis, here is the kind of material to use." He took a clipping from his wallet and slapped it on the bar.

"ADDING MACHINE USED IN RITUAL OF WESTERN SECT . . .
Figures Will Be Used for Prayers for Condemned Slayer of Aged Recluse. . . . DENVER, COLO., Feb. 2 (A. P.) Frank H. Rice, Supreme Pontiff of the Liberal Church of America has announced he will carry out his plan for a 'goat and adding machine' ritual for William Moya, condemned slayer, despite objection to his program by a Cardinal of the sect. Rice declared the goat would be used as part of a 'sack cloth and ashes' service shortly before and after Moya's execution, set for the week of June 20. Prayers for the condemned man's soul will be offered on an adding machine. Numbers, he explained, constitute the only universal language. Moya killed Joseph Zemp, an aged recluse, in an argument over a small amount of money."

Miss Farkis laughed and Shrike raised his fist as though to strike her. His actions shocked the bartender, who hurriedly asked them to go into the back room. Miss Lonelyhearts did not want to go along, but Shrike insisted and he was too tired to argue.

They seated themselves at a table inside one of the booths. Shrike again raised his fist, but when Miss Farkis drew back, he changed the gesture to a caress. The trick worked. She gave in to his hand until he became too daring, then pushed him away.

Shrike again began to shout and this time Miss

Lonelyhearts understood that he was making a se-
duction speech.

"I am a great saint," Shrike cried, "I can walk on
my own water. Haven't you ever heard of Shrike's
Passion in the Luncheonette, or the Agony in the
Soda Fountain? Then I compared the wounds in
Christ's body to the mouths of a miraculous purse in
which we deposit the small change of our sins. It is
indeed an excellent conceit. But now let us consider
the holes in our own bodies and into what these con-
genital wounds open. Under the skin of man is a
wondrous jungle where veins like lush tropical
growths hang along over-ripe organs and weed-like
entrails writhe in squirming tangles of red and yellow. In this jungle, flitting from rock-gray lungs to
golden intestines, from liver to lights and back to
liver again, lives a bird called the soul. The Catholic
hunts this bird with bread and wine, the Hebrew
with a golden ruler, the Protestant on leaden feet
with leaden words, the Buddhist with gestures, the
Negro with blood. I spit on them all. Phooh! And I
call upon you to spit. Phooh! Do you stuff birds? No,
my dears, taxidermy is not religion. No! A thousand
times no. Better, I say unto you, better a live bird in
the jungle of the body than two stuffed birds on the
library table."

His caresses kept pace with the sermon. When he
had reached the end, he buried his triangular face
like the blade of a hatchet in her neck.

Miss Lonelyhearts

and the Lamb

MISS LONELYHEARTS went home in a taxi. He lived by himself in a room that was full of shadows as an old steel engraving. It held a bed, a table and two chairs. The walls were bare except for an ivory Christ that hung opposite the foot of the bed. He had removed the figure from the cross to which it had been fastened and had nailed it to the wall with large spikes. But the desired effect had not been obtained. Instead of writhing, the Christ remained calmly decorative.

He got undressed immediately and took a cigarette and a copy of *The Brothers Karamazov* to bed. The marker was in a chapter devoted to Father Zossima.

"Love a man even in his sin, for that is the semblance of Divine Love and is the highest love on earth. Love all God's creation, the whole and every grain of sand in it. Love the animals, love the plants, love everything. If you love everything, you will perceive the divine mystery in things. Once you perceive it, you will begin to comprehend it better every day. And you will come at last to love the whole world with an all-embracing love."

It was excellent advice. If he followed it, he would be a big success. His column would be syndicated and the whole world would learn to love. The Kingdom of Heaven would arrive. He would sit on the right hand of the Lamb.

But seriously, he realized, even if Shrike had not made a sane view of this Christ business impossible, there would be little use in his fooling himself. His vocation was of a different sort. As a boy in his father's church, he had discovered that something stirred in him when he shouted the name of Christ, something secret and enormously powerful. He had played with this thing, but had never allowed it to come alive.

He knew now what this thing was—hysteria, a snake whose scales are tiny mirrors in which the dead world takes on a semblance of life. And how dead the world is . . . a world of doorknobs. He wondered if hysteria were really too steep a price to pay for bringing it to life.

For him, Christ was the most natural of excitements. Fixing his eyes on the image that hung on the wall, he began to chant: "Christ, Christ, Jesus Christ. Christ, Christ, Jesus Christ." But the moment the snake started to uncoil in his brain, he became frightened and closed his eyes.

With sleep, a dream came in which he found himself on the stage of a crowded theater. He was a magician who did tricks with doorknobs. At his command, they bled, flowered, spoke. After his act was finished, he tried to lead his audience in prayer. But no matter how hard he struggled, his prayer was one Shrike had taught him and his voice was that of a conductor calling stations.

"Oh, Lord, we are not of those who wash in wine, water, urine, vinegar, fire, oil, bay rum, milk, brandy, or boric acid. Oh, Lord, we are of those who wash solely in the Blood of the Lamb."

The scene of the dream changed. He found himself in his college dormitory. With him were Steve Garvey and Jud Hume. They had been arguing the existence of God from midnight until dawn, and now, having run out of whisky, they decided to go to the market for some applejack.

Their way led through the streets of the sleeping town into the open fields beyond. It was spring. The sun and the smell of vegetable birth renewed their drunkenness and they reeled between the loaded carts. The farmers took their horseplay good-naturedly. Boys from the college on a spree.

They found the bootlegger and bought a gallon jug of applejack, then wandered to the section where livestock was sold. They stopped to fool with some lambs. Jud suggested buying one to roast over a fire in the woods. Miss Lonelyhearts agreed, but on the condition that they sacrifice it to God before barbecuing it.

Steve was sent to the cutlery stand for a butcher knife, while the other two remained to bargain for a lamb. After a long, Armenian-like argument, during which Jud exhibited his farm training, the youngest was selected, a little, stiff-legged thing, all head.

They paraded the lamb through the market. Miss Lonelyhearts went first, carrying the knife, the others followed, Steve with the jug and Jud with the animal. As they marched, they sang an obscene version of "Mary Had a Little Lamb."

Between the market and the hill on which they intended to perform the sacrifice was a meadow. While going through it, they picked daisies and buttercups. Halfway up the hill, they found a rock and covered it with the flowers. They laid the lamb among the flowers. Miss Lonelyhearts was elected priest, with Steve and Jud as his attendants. While they held the lamb, Miss Lonelyhearts crouched over it and began to chant.

"Christ, Christ, Jesus Christ. Christ, Christ, Jesus Christ."

When they had worked themselves into a frenzy, he brought the knife down hard. The blow was inaccurate and made a flesh wound. He raised the knife again and this time the lamb's violent struggles made him miss altogether. The knife broke on the altar. Steve and Jud pulled the animal's head back for him to saw at its throat, but only a small piece of blade remained in the handle and he was unable to cut through the matted wool.

Their hands were covered with slimy blood and the lamb slipped free. It crawled off into the underbrush.

As the bright sun outlined the altar rock with narrow shadows, the scene appeared to gather itself for some new violence. They bolted. Down the hill they fled until they reached the meadow, where they fell exhausted in the tall grass.

After some time had passed, Miss Lonelyhearts begged them to go back and put the lamb out of its misery. They refused to go. He went back alone and found it under a bush. He crushed its head with a stone and left the carcass to the flies that swarmed around the bloody altar flowers.

Miss Lonelyhearts

and the Fat Thumb

MISS LONELYHEARTS found himself developing an almost insane sensitiveness to order. Everything had to form a pattern: the shoes under the bed, the ties in the holder, the pencils on the table. When he looked out of a window, he composed the skyline by balancing one building against another. If a bird flew across this arrangement, he closed his eyes angrily until it was gone.

For a little while, he seemed to hold his own but one day he found himself with his back to the wall. On that day all the inanimate things over which he had tried to obtain control took the field against him. When he touched something, it spilled or rolled to the floor. The collar buttons disappeared under the bed, the point of the pencil broke, the handle of the razor fell off, the window shade refused to stay down. He fought back, but with too much violence, and was decisively defeated by the spring of the alarm clock.

He fled to the street, but there chaos was multiple. Broken groups of people hurried past, forming neither stars nor squares. The lamp-posts were badly spaced and the flagging was of different sizes. Nor could he do anything with the harsh clanging sound of street cars and the raw shouts of hucksters. No repeated group of words would fit their rhythm and no scale could give them meaning.

He stood quietly against a wall, trying not to see or hear. Then he remembered Betty. She had often made him feel that when she straightened his tie, she straightened much more. And he had once thought that if her world were larger, were *the* world, she might order it as finally as the objects on her dressing table.

He gave Betty's address to a cab driver and told him to hurry. But she lived on the other side of the city and by the time he got there, his panic had turned to irritation.

She came to the door of her apartment in a crisp, white linen dressing-robe that yellowed into brown at the edges. She held out both her hands to him and her arms showed round and smooth like wood that has been turned by the sea.

With the return of self-consciousness, he knew that only violence could make him supple. It was Betty, however, that he criticized. Her world was not the world and could never include the readers of his column. Her sureness was based on the power to limit experience arbitrarily. Moreover, his confusion was significant, while her order was not.

He tried to reply to her greeting and discovered that his tongue had become a fat thumb. To avoid talking, he awkwardly forced a kiss, then found it necessary to apologize.

"Too much lover's return business, I know, and I . . ." He stumbled purposely, so that she would take his confusion for honest feeling. But the trick failed and she waited for him to continue:

"Please eat dinner with me."

"I'm afraid I can't."

Her smile opened into a laugh.

She was laughing at him. On the defense, he examined her laugh for "bitterness," "sour-grapes," "a-broken-heart," "the devil-may-care." But to his confusion, he found nothing at which to laugh back. Her smile had opened naturally, not like an umbrella, and while he watched her laugh folded and became a smile again, a smile that was neither "wry," "ironical" nor "mysterious."

As they moved into the living-room, his irritation increased. She sat down on a studio couch with her bare legs under and her back straight. Behind her a silver tree flowered in the lemon wall-paper. He remained standing.

"Betty the Buddha," he said. "Betty the Buddha. You have the smug smile; all you need is the pot belly."

His voice was so full of hatred that he himself was surprised. He fidgeted for a while in silence and finally sat down beside her on the couch to take her hand.

More than two months had passed since he had sat with her on this same couch and had asked her to marry him. Then she had accepted him and they had planned their life after marriage, his job and her gingham apron, his slippers beside the fireplace and her ability to cook. He had avoided her since. He did not feel guilty; he was merely annoyed at having been fooled into thinking that such a solution was possible.

He soon grew tired of holding hands and began to fidget again. He remembered that towards the end of his last visit he had put his hand inside her clothes. Unable to think of anything else to do, he now repeated the gesture. She was naked under her robe and he found her breast.

She made no sign to show that she was aware of his hand. He would have welcomed a slap, but even when he caught at her nipple, she remained silent.

"Let me pluck this rose," he said, giving a sharp tug. "I want to wear it in my buttonhole."

Betty reached for his brow. "What's the matter?" she asked. "Are you sick?"

He began to shout at her, accompanying his shouts with gestures that were too appropriate, like those of an old-fashioned actor.

"What a kind bitch you are. As soon as any one acts viciously, you say he's sick. Wife-torturers, rapers of small children, according to you they're all sick. No morality, only medicine. Well, I'm not sick. I don't need any of your damned aspirin. I've got a Christ complex. Humanity ... I'm a humanity lover. All the broken bastards ..." He finished with a short laugh that was like a bark.

She had left the couch for a red chair that was swollen with padding and tense with live springs.

In the lap of this leather monster, all trace of the serene Buddha disappeared.

But his anger was not appeased. "What's the matter, sweetheart?" he asked, patting her shoulder threateningly. "Didn't you like the performance?"

Instead of answering, she raised her arm as though to ward off a blow. She was like a kitten whose soft helplessness makes one ache to hurt it.

"What's the matter?" he demanded over and over again. "What's the matter? What's the matter?"

Her face took on the expression of an inexperienced gambler about to venture all on a last throw. He was turning for his hat, when she spoke.

"I love you."

"You what?"

The need for repeating flustered her, yet she managed to keep her manner undramatic.

"I love you."

"And I love you," he said. "You and your damned smiling through tears."

"Why don't you let me alone?" She had begun to cry. "I felt swell before you came, and now I feel lousy. Go away. Please go away."

Miss Lonelyhearts

and the Clean Old Man

IN THE STREET AGAIN, Miss Lonelyhearts wondered what to do next. He was too excited to eat and afraid to go home. He felt as though his heart were a bomb, a complicated bomb that would result in a simple explosion, wrecking the world without rocking it.

He decided to go to Delehanty's for a drink. In the speakeasy, he discovered a group of his friends at the bar. They greeted him and went on talking. One of them was complaining about the number of female writers.

"And they've all got three names," he said. "Mary Roberts Wilcox, Ella Wheeler Catheter, Ford Mary Rinehart. . . ."

Then some one started a train of stories by suggesting that what they all needed was a good rape.

"I knew a gal who was regular until she fell in

with a group and went literary. She began writing for the little magazines about how much Beauty hurt her and ditched the boy friend who set up pins in a bowling alley. The guys on the block got sore and took her into the lots one night. About eight of them. They ganged her proper...."

"That's like the one they tell about another female writer. When this hard-boiled stuff first came in, she dropped the trick English accent and went in for scram and lam. She got to hanging around with a lot of mugs in a speak, gathering material for a novel. Well, the mugs didn't know they were picturesque and thought she was regular until the barkeep put them wise. They got her into the back room to teach her a new word and put the boots to her. They didn't let her out for three days. On the last day they sold tickets to niggers...."

Miss Lonelyhearts stopped listening. His friends would go on telling these stories until they were too drunk to talk. They were aware of their childishness, but did not know how else to revenge themselves. At college, and perhaps for a year afterwards, they had believed in literature, had believed in Beauty and in personal expression as an absolute end. When they lost this belief, they lost everything. Money and fame meant nothing to them. They were not worldly men.

Miss Lonelyhearts drank steadily. He was smiling an innocent, amused smile, the smile of an anarchist sitting in the movies with a bomb in his pocket. If the people around him only knew what was in his pocket. In a little while he would leave to kill the President.

Not until he heard his own name mentioned did he stop smiling and again begin to listen.

"He's a leper licker. Shrike says he wants to lick lepers, Barkeep, a leper for the gent."

"If you haven't got a leper, give him a Hungarian."

"Well, that's the trouble with his approach to God. It's too damn literary—plain song, Latin poetry, medieval painting, Huysmans, stained-glass windows and crap like that."

"Even if he were to have a genuine religious experience, it would be personal and so meaningless, except to a psychologist."

"The trouble with him, the trouble with all of us, is that we have no outer life, only an inner one, and that by necessity."

"He's an escapist. He wants to cultivate his interior garden. But you can't escape, and where is he going to find a market for the fruits of his personality? The Farm Board is a failure."

"What I say is, after all one has to earn a living. We can't all believe in Christ, and what does the farmer care about art? He takes his shoes off to get the warm feel of the rich earth between his toes. You can't take your shoes off in church."

Miss Lonelyhearts had again begun to smile. Like Shrike, the man they imitated, they were machines for making jokes. A button machine makes buttons, no matter what the power used, foot, steam or electricity. They, no matter what the motivating force, death, love or God, made jokes.

"Was their nonsense the only barrier?" he asked

himself. "Had he been thwarted by such a low
hurdle?"

The whisky was good and he felt warm and sure.
Through the light-blue tobacco smoke, the mahogany bar shone like wet gold. The glasses and bottles,
their high lights exploding, rang like a battery of
little bells when the bartender touched them together. He forgot that his heart was a bomb to remember an incident of his childhood. One winter
evening, he had been waiting with his little sister for
their father to come home from church. She was
eight years old then, and he was twelve. Made sad
by the pause between playing and eating, he had
gone to the piano and had begun a piece by Mozart.
It was the first time he had ever voluntarily gone
to the piano. His sister left her picture book to
dance to his music. She had never danced before.
She danced gravely and carefully, a simple dance yet
formal. . . . As Miss Lonelyhearts stood at the bar,
swaying slightly to the remembered music, he
thought of children dancing. Square replacing ob-
long and being replaced by circle. Every child, everywhere; in the whole world there was not one
child who was not gravely, sweetly dancing.

He stepped away from the bar and accidentally
collided with a man holding a glass of beer. When he
turned to beg the man's pardon, he received a punch
in the mouth. Later he found himself at a table in the
back room, playing with a loose tooth. He wondered
why his hat did not fit and discovered a lump on
the back of his head. He must have fallen. The hurdle was higher than he had thought.

His anger swung in large drunken circles. What in

Christ's name was this Christ business? And children gravely dancing? He would ask Shrike to be transferred to the sports department.

Ned Gates came in to see how he was getting along and suggested the fresh air. Gates was also very drunk. When they left the speakeasy together, they found that it was snowing.

Miss Lonelyhearts' anger grew cold and sodden like the snow. He and his companion staggered along with their heads down, turning corners at random, until they found themselves in front of the little park. A light was burning in the comfort station and they went in to warm up.

An old man was sitting on one of the toilets. The door of his booth was propped open and he was sitting on the turned-down toilet cover.

Gates hailed him. "Well, well, snug as a bug in a rug, eh?"

The old man jumped with fright, but finally managed to speak. "What do you want? Please let me alone." His voice was like a flute; it did not vibrate.

"If you can't get a woman, get a clean old man," Gates sang.

The old man looked as if he were going to cry, but suddenly laughed instead. A terrible cough started under his laugh, and catching at the bottom of his lungs, it ripped into his throat. He turned away to wipe his mouth.

Miss Lonelyhearts tried to get Gates to leave, but he refused to go without the old man. They both grabbed him and pulled him out of the stall and through the door of the comfort station. He went soft in their arms and started to giggle. Miss Lonelyhearts fought off a desire to hit him.

The snow had stopped falling and it had grown very cold. The old man did not have an overcoat, but said that he found the cold exhilarating. He carried a cane and wore gloves because, as he said, he detested red hands.

Instead of going back to Delehanty's, they went to an Italian cellar close to the park. The old man tried to get them to drink coffee, but they told him to mind his own business and drank rye. The whisky burned Miss Lonelyhearts' cut lip.

Gates was annoyed by the old man's elaborate manners. "Listen, you," he said, "cut out the gentlemanly stuff and tell us the story of your life."

The old man drew himself up like a little girl making a muscle.

"Aw, come off," Gates said. "We're scientists. He's Havelock Ellis and I'm Krafft-Ebing. When did you first discover homosexualistic tendencies in yourself?"

"What do you mean, sir? I . . ."

"Yeh, I know, but how about your difference from other men?"

"How dare you . . ." He gave a little scream of indignation.

"Now, now," Miss Lonelyhearts said, "he didn't mean to insult you. Scientists have terribly bad manners. . . . But you are a pervert, aren't you?"

The old man raised his cane to strike him. Gates grabbed it from behind and wrenched it out of his hand. He began to cough violently and held his black satin tie to his mouth. Still coughing he dragged himself to a chair in the back of the room.

Miss Lonelyhearts felt as he had felt years before, when he had accidentally stepped on a small frog. Its spilled guts had filled him with pity, but when its suffering had become real to his senses, his pity had turned to rage and he had beaten it frantically until it was dead.

"I'll get the bastard's life story," he shouted, and started after him. Gates following laughing.

At their approach, the old man jumped to his feet. Miss Lonelyhearts caught him and forced him back into the chair.

"We're psychologists," he said, "We want to help you. What's your name?"

"George B. Simpson."

"What does the B stand for?"

"Bramhall."

"Your age, please, and the nature of your quest?"

"By what right do you ask?"

"Science gives me the right."

"Let's drop it," Gates said. "The old fag is going to cry."

"No, Krafft-Ebing, sentiment must never be permitted to interfere with the probings of science."

Miss Lonelyhearts put his arm around the old man. "Tell us the story of your life," he said, loading his voice with sympathy.

"I have no story."

"You must have. Every one has a life story."

The old man began to sob.

"Yes, I know, your tale is a sad one. Tell it, damn you, tell it."

When the old man still remained silent, he took his arm and twisted it. Gates tried to tear him away, but he refused to let go. He was twisting the arm of all the sick and miserable, broken and betrayed, inarticulate and impotent. He was twisting the arm of Desperate, Broken-hearted, Sick-of-it-all, Disillusioned-with-tubercular-husband.

The old man began to scream. Somebody hit Miss Lonelyhearts from behind with a chair.

Miss Lonelyhearts

and Mrs. Shrike

MISS LONELYHEARTS lay on his bed fully dressed, just as he had been dumped the night before. His head ached and his thoughts revolved inside the pain like a wheel within a wheel. When he opened his eyes, the room, like a third wheel, revolved around the pain in his head.

From where he lay he could see the alarm clock. It was half past three. When the telephone rang, he crawled out of the sour pile of bed clothes. Shrike wanted to know if he intended to show up at the office. He answered that he was drunk but would try to get there.

He undressed slowly and took a bath. The hot water made his body feel good, but his heart remained a congealed lump of icy fat. After drying himself, he found a little whisky in the medicine chest and drank it. The alcohol warmed only the lining of his stomach.

He shaved, put on a clean shirt and a freshly pressed suit and went out to get something to eat. When he had finished his second cup of scalding coffee, it was too late for him to go to work. But he had nothing to worry about, for Shrike would never fire him. He made too perfect a butt for Shrike's jokes. Once he had tried to get fired by recommending suicide in his column. All that Shrike had said was: "Remember, please, that your job is to increase the circulation of our paper. Suicide, it is only reasonable to think, must defeat this purpose."

He paid for his breakfast and left the cafeteria. Some exercise might warm him. He decided to take a brisk walk, but he soon grew tired and when he reached the little park, he slumped down on a bench opposite the Mexican War obelisk.

The stone shaft cast a long, rigid shadow on the walk in front of him. He sat staring at it without knowing why until he noticed that it was lengthening in rapid jerks, not as shadows usually lengthen. He grew frightened and looked up quickly at the monument. It seemed red and swollen in the dying sun, as though it were about to spout a load of granite seed.

He hurried away. When he had regained the street, he started to laugh. Although he had tried hot water, whisky, coffee, exercise, he had completely forgotten sex. What he really needed was a woman. He laughed again, remembering that at college all his friends had believed intercourse capable of steadying the nerves, relaxing the muscles and clearing the blood.

But he knew only two women who would tolerate him. He had spoiled his chances with Betty, so it would have to be Mary Shrike.

When he kissed Shrike's wife, he felt less like a joke. She returned his kisses because she hated Shrike. But even there Shrike had beaten him. No matter how hard he begged her to give Shrike horns, she refused to sleep with him.

Although Mary always grunted and upset her eyes, she would not associate what she felt with the sexual act. When he forced this association, she became very angry. He had been convinced that her grunts were genuine by the change that took place in her when he kissed her heavily. Then her body gave off an odor that enriched the synthetic flower scent she used behind her ears and in the hollows of her neck. No similar change ever took place in his own body, however. Like a dead man, only friction could make him warm or violence make him mobile.

He decided to get a few drinks and then call Mary from Delehanty's. It was quite early and the speakeasy was empty. The bartender served him and went back to his newspaper.

On the mirror behind the bar hung a poster advertising a mineral water. It showed a naked girl made modest by the mist that rose from the spring at her feet. The artist had taken a great deal of care in drawing her breasts and their nipples stuck out like tiny red hats.

He tried to excite himself into eagerness by thinking of the play Mary made with her breasts. She used them as the coquettes of long ago had used their fans. One of her tricks was to wear a medal low down on her chest. Whenever he asked to see it, instead of drawing it out she leaned over for him to look. Although he had often asked to see the medal, he had not yet found out what it represented.

But the excitement refused to come. If anything, he felt colder than before he had started to think of women. It was not his line. Nevertheless, he persisted in it, out of desperation, and went to the telephone to call Mary.

"Is that you?" she asked, then added before he could reply, "I must see you at once. I've quarreled with him. This time I'm through."

She always talked in headlines and her excitement forced him to be casual. "O.K.," he said. "When? Where?"

"Anywhere, I'm through with that skunk, I tell you, I'm through."

She had quarreled with Shrike before and he knew that in return for an ordinary number of kisses, he would have to listen to an extraordinary amount of complaining.

"Do you want to meet me here, in Delehanty's?" he asked.

"No, you come here. We'll be alone and anyway I have to bathe and get dressed."

When he arrived at her place, he would probably find Shrike there with her on his lap. They would both be glad to see him and all three of them would go to the movies where Mary would hold his hand under the seat.

He went back to the bar for another drink, then

bought a quart of Scotch and took a cab. Shrike opened the door. Although he had expected to see him, he was embarrassed and tried to cover his confusion by making believe that he was extremely drunk.

"Come in, come in, homebreaker," Shrike said with a laugh. "The Mrs. will be out in a few minutes. She's in the tub."

Shrike took the bottle he was carrying and pulled its cork. Then he got some charged water and made two highballs.

"Well," Shrike said, lifting his drink, "so you're going in for this kind of stuff, eh? Whisky and the boss's wife."

Miss Lonelyhearts always found it impossible to reply to him. The answers he wanted to make were too general and began too far back in the history of their relationship.

"You're doing field work, I take it," Shrike said. "Well, don't put this whisky on your expense account. However, we like to see a young man with his heart in his work. You've been going around with yours in your mouth."

Miss Lonelyhearts made a desperate attempt to kid back. "And you," he said, "you're an old meanie who beats his wife."

Shrike laughed, but too long and too loudly, then broke off with an elaborate sigh. "Ah, my lad," he said, "you're wrong. It's Mary who does the beating."

He took a long pull at his highball and sighed again, still more elaborately. "My good friend, I want to have a heart-to-heart talk with you. I adore heart-to-heart talks and nowadays there are so few people with whom one can really talk. Everybody is so hard-boiled. I want to make a clean breast of matters, a nice clean breast. It's better to make a clean breast of matters than to let them fester in the depths of one's soul."

While talking, he kept his face alive with little nods and winks that were evidently supposed to inspire confidence and to prove him a very simple fellow.

"My good friend, your accusation hurts me to the quick. You spiritual lovers think that you alone suffer. But you are mistaken. Although my love is of the flesh flashy, I too suffer. It's suffering that drives me into the arms of the Miss Farkises of this world. Yes, I suffer."

Here the dead pan broke and pain actually crept into his voice. "She's selfish. She's a damned selfish bitch. She was a virgin when I married her and has been fighting ever since to remain one. Sleeping with her is like sleeping with a knife in one's groin."

It was Miss Lonelyhearts' turn to laugh. He put his face close to Shrike's and laughed as hard as he could.

Shrike tried to ignore him by finishing as though the whole thing were a joke.

"She claims that I raped her. Can you imagine Willie Shrike, wee Willie Shrike, raping any one? I'm like you, one of those grateful lovers."

Mary came into the room in her bathrobe. She leaned over Miss Lonelyhearts and said: "Don't talk to that pig. Come with me and bring the whisky."

As he followed her into the bedroom, he heard Shrike slam the front door. She went into a large closet to dress. He sat on the bed.

"What did that swine say to you?"

"He said you were selfish, Mary—sexually selfish."

"Of all the god-damned nerve. Do you know why he lets me go out with other men? To save money. He knows that I let them neck me and when I get home all hot and bothered, why he climbs into my bed and begs for it. The cheap bastard!"

She came out of the closet wearing a black lace slip and began to fix her hair in front of the dressing table. Miss Lonelyhearts bent down to kiss the back of her neck.

"Now, now," she said, acting kittenish, "you'll muss me."

He took a drink from the whisky bottle, then made her a highball. When he brought it to her, she gave him a kiss, a little peck of reward.

"Where'll we eat?" she asked. "Let's go where we can dance. I want to be gay."

They took a cab to a place called El Gaucho. When they entered, the orchestra was playing a Cuban rhumba. A waiter dressed as a South-American cowboy led them to a table. Mary immediately went Spanish and her movements became languorous and full of abandon.

But the romantic atmosphere only heightened his feeling of icy fatness. He tried to fight it by telling himself that it was childish. What had happened to his great understanding heart? Guitars, bright shawls, exotic foods, outlandish costumes—all these things were part of the business of dreams. He had learned not to laugh at the advertisements offering to teach writing, cartooning, engineering, to add inches to the biceps and to develop the bust. He should therefore realize that the people who came to El Gaucho were the same as those who wanted to write and live the life of an artist, wanted to be an engineer and wear leather puttees, wanted to develop a grip that would impress the boss, wanted to cushion Raoul's head on their swollen breasts. They were the same people as those who wrote to Miss Lonelyhearts for help.

But his irritation was too profound for him to soothe it in this way. For the time being, dreams left him cold, no matter how humble they were.

"I like this place," Mary said. "It's a little fakey, I know, but it's gay and I so want to be gay."

She thanked him by offering herself in a series of formal, impersonal gestures. She was wearing a tight, shiny dress that was like glass-covered steel and there was something cleanly mechanical in her pantomime.

"Why do you want to be gay?"

"Every one wants to be gay—unless they're sick."

Was he sick? In a great cold wave, the readers of his column crashed over the music, over the bright shawls and picturesque waiters, over her shining body. To save himself, he asked to see the medal. Like a little girl helping an old man to cross the street, she leaned over for him to look into the neck of her dress. But before he had a chance to see anything, a waiter came up to the table.

"The way to be gay is to make other people gay," Miss Lonelyhearts said. "Sleep with me and I'll be one gay dog."

The defeat in his voice made it easy for her to ignore his request and her mind sagged with his.

"I've had a tough time," she said. "From the beginning, I've had a tough time. When I was a child, I saw my mother die. She had cancer of the breast and the pain was terrible. She died leaning over a table."

"Sleep with me," he said.

"No, let's dance."

"I don't want to. Tell me about your mother."

"She died leaning over a table. The pain was so terrible that she climbed out of bed to die."

Mary leaned over to show how her mother had died and he made another attempt to see the medal. He saw that there was a runner on it, but was unable to read the inscription.

"My father was very cruel to her," she continued. "He was a portrait painter, a man of genius, but..."

He stopped listening and tried to bring his great understanding heart into action again. Parents are also part of the business of dreams. My father was a Russian prince, my father was a Piute Indian chief, my father was an Australian sheep baron, my father lost all his money in Wall Street, my father was a portrait painter. People like Mary were unable to do without such tales. They told them because they wanted to talk about something besides clothing or business or the movies, because they wanted to talk about something poetic.

When she had finished her story, he said, "You poor kid," and leaned over for another look at the medal. She bent to help him and pulled out the neck of her dress with her fingers. This time he was able to read the inscription: "Awarded by the Boston Latin School for first place in the 100 yd. dash."

It was a small victory, yet it greatly increased his fatigue and he was glad when she suggested leaving. In the cab, he again begged her to sleep with him. She refused. He kneaded her body like a sculptor grown angry with his clay, but there was too much method in his caresses and they both remained cold.

At the door of her apartment, she turned for a kiss and pressed against him. A spark flared up in his groin. He refused to let go and tried to work this spark into a flame. She pushed his mouth away from a long wet kiss.

"Listen to me," she said. "We can't stop talking. We must talk. Willie probably heard the elevator and is listening behind the door. You don't know him. If he doesn't hear us talk, he'll know you're kissing me and open the door. It's an old trick of his."

He held her close and tried desperately to keep the spark alive.

"Don't kiss my lips," she begged. "I must talk."

He kissed her throat, then opened her dress and kissed her breasts. She was afraid to resist or to stop talking.

"My mother died of cancer of the breast," she said in a brave voice, like a little girl reciting at a party. "She died leaning over a table. My father was a portrait painter. He led a very gay life. He mistreated my mother. She had cancer of the breast. She . . ." He tore at her clothes and she began to mumble and repeat herself. Her dress fell to her feet and he tore away her underwear until she was naked under her fur coat. He tried to drag her to the floor.

"Please, please," she begged, "he'll come out and find us."

He stopped her mouth with a long kiss.

"Let me go, honey," she pleaded, "maybe he's not home. If he isn't, I'll let you in."

He released her. She opened the door and tiptoed in, carrying her rolled up clothes under her coat. He heard her switch on the light in the foyer and knew that Shrike had not been behind the door. Then he heard footsteps and limped behind a projection of the elevator shaft. The door opened and Shrike looked into the corridor. He had on only the top of his pajamas.

Miss Lonelyhearts

on a Field Trip

IT WAS COLD AND DAMP in the city room the next day, and Miss Lonelyhearts sat at his desk with his hands in his pockets and his legs pressed together. A desert, he was thinking, not of sand, but of rust and body dirt, surrounded by a back-yard fence on which are posters describing the events of the day. Mother slays five with ax, slays seven, slays nine.... Babe slams two, slams three.... Inside the fence Desperate, Broken-hearted, Disillusioned-with-tuber-cular-husband and the rest were gravely forming the letters MISS LONELYHEARTS out of white-washed clam shells, as if decorating the lawn of a rural depot.

He failed to notice Goldsmith's waddling approach until a heavy arm dropped on his neck like the arm of a deadfall. He freed himself with a grunt. His anger amused Goldsmith, who smiled, bunching his fat cheeks like twin rolls of smooth pink toilet paper.

"Well, how's the drunkard?" Goldsmith asked, imitating Shrike.

Miss Lonelyhearts knew that Goldsmith had written the column for him yesterday, so he hid his annoyance to be grateful.

"No trouble at all," Goldsmith said. "It was a pleasure to read your mail." He took a pink envelope out of his pocket and threw it on the desk "From an admirer." He winked, letting a thick gray lid down slowly and luxuriously over a moist, rolling eye.

Miss Lonelyhearts picked up the letter.

Dear Miss Lonelyhearts—

I am not very good at writing so I wonder if I could have a talk with you. I am only 32 years old but have had a lot of trouble in my life and am unhappily married to a cripple. I need some good advice bad but can't state my case in a letter as I am not good at letters and it would take an expert to state my case. I know your a man and am glad as I dont trust women. You were pointed out to me in Delehantys as the man who does the advice in the paper and the minute I saw you I said you can help me. You had on a blue suit and a gray hat when I came in with my husband who is a cripple.

I dont feel so bad about asking you to see you personal because I feel almost like I knew you. So please call me up at Burgess 7-7323 which is my number as I need your advice bad about my married life.

An admirer,
Fay Doyle

He threw the letter into the waste-paper basket with a great show of distaste.

Goldsmith laughed at him. "How now, Dostoevski?" he said. "That's no way to act. Instead of pulling the Russian by recommending suicide, you ought to get the lady with child and increase the potential circulation of the paper."

To drive him away, Miss Lonelyhearts made believe that he was busy. He went over to his typewriter and started pounding out his column.

"Life, for most of us, seems a terrible struggle of pain and heartbreak, without hope or joy. Oh, my dear readers, it only seems so. Every man, no matter how poor or humble, can teach himself to use his senses. See the cloud-flecked sky, the foam-decked sea. . . . Smell the sweet pine and heady privet. . . . Feel of velvet and of satin. . . . As the popular song goes, 'The best things in life are free.' Life is . . ."

He could not go on with it and turned again to the imagined desert where Desperate, Broken-hearted and the others were still building his name. They had run out of sea shells and were using faded photographs, soiled fans, time-tables, playing cards, broken toys, imitation jewelry—junk that memory had made precious, far more precious than anything the sea might yield.

He killed his great understanding heart by laughing, then reached into the waste-paper basket for Mrs. Doyle's letter. Like a pink tent, he set it over the desert. Against the dark mahogany desk top, the cheap paper took on rich flesh tones. He thought of Mrs. Doyle as a tent, hair-covered and veined, and of himself as the skeleton in a water closet, the

skull and cross-bones on a scholar's bookplate. When
he made the skeleton enter the flesh tent, it flowered
at every joint.

But despite these thoughts, he remained as dry
and cold as a polished bone and sat trying to discover
a moral reason for not calling Mrs. Doyle. If he could
only believe in Christ, then adultery would be a sin,
then everything would be simple and the letters extremely easy to answer.

The completeness of his failure drove him to the
telephone. He left the city room and went into the
hall to use the pay station from which all private
calls had to be made. The walls of the booth were
covered with obscene drawings. He fastened his
eyes on two disembodied genitals and gave the op-
erator Burgess 7-7323.

"Is Mrs. Doyle in?"

"Hello, who is it?"

"I want to speak to Mrs. Doyle," he said. "Is this
Mrs. Doyle?"

"Yes, that's me." Her voice was hard with fright.

"This is Miss Lonelyhearts."

"Miss who?"

"Miss Lonelyhearts, Miss Lonelyhearts, the man
who does the column."

He was about to hang up, when she cooed, "Oh,
hello. . . ."

"You said I should call."

"Oh, yes . . . what?"

He guessed that she wanted him to do the talking.
"When can you see me?"

"Now." She was still cooing and he could almost

feel her warm, moisture-laden breath through the earpiece.

"Where?"

"You say."

"I'll tell you what," he said. "Meet me in the park, near the obelisk, in about an hour."

He went back to his desk and finished his column, then started for the park. He sat down on a bench near the obelisk to wait for Mrs. Doyle. Still thinking of tents, he examined the sky and saw that it was canvas-colored and ill-stretched. He examined it like a stupid detective who is searching for a clue to his own exhaustion. When he found nothing, he turned his trained eye on the skyscrapers that menaced the little park from all sides. In their tons of forced rock and tortured steel, he discovered what he thought was a clue.

Americans have dissipated their racial energy in an orgy of stone breaking. In their few years they have broken more stones than did centuries of Egyptians. And they have done their work hysterically, desperately, almost as if they knew that the stones would some day break them.

The detective saw a big woman enter the park and start in his direction. He made a quick catalogue: legs like Indian clubs, breasts like balloons and a brow like a pigeon. Despite her short plaid skirt, red sweater, rabbit-skin jacket and knitted tam-o'-shanter, she looked like a police captain.

He waited for her to speak first.

"Miss Lonelyhearts? Oh, hello . . ."

"Mrs. Doyle?" He stood up and took her arm. It felt like a thigh.

"Where are we going?" she asked, as he began to lead her off.

"For a drink."

"I can't go to Delehanty's. They know me."

"We'll go to my place."

"Ought I?"

He did not have to answer, for she was already on her way. As he followed her up the stairs to his apartment, he watched the action of her massive hams; they were like two enormous grindstones.

He made some highballs and sat down beside her on the bed.

"You must know an awful lot about women from your job," she said with a sigh, putting her hand on his knee.

He had always been the pursuer, but now found a strange pleasure in having the rôles reversed. He drew back when she reached for a kiss. She caught his head and kissed him on his mouth. At first it ticked like a watch, then the tick softened and thickened into a heart throb. It beat louder and more rapidly each second, until he thought that it was going to explode and pulled away with a rude jerk.

"Don't," she begged.

"Don't what?"

"Oh, darling, turn out the light."

He smoked a cigarette, standing in the dark and listening to her undress. She made sea sounds; something flapped like a sail; there was the creak of ropes; then he heard the wave-against-a-wharf smack of rubber on flesh. Her call for him to hurry was a sea-moan, and when he lay beside her, she heaved, tidal, moon-driven.

Some fifteen minutes later, he crawled out of bed like an exhausted swimmer leaving the surf, and dropped down into a large armchair near the window. She went into the bathroom, then came back and sat in his lap.

"I'm ashamed of myself," she said. "You must think I'm a bad woman."

He shook his head no.

"My husband isn't much. He's a cripple like I wrote you, and much older than me." She laughed. "He's all dried up. He hasn't been a husband to me for years. You know, Lucy, my kid, isn't his."

He saw that she expected him to be astonished and did his best to lift his eyebrows.

"It's a long story," she said. "It was on account of Lucy that I had to marry him. I'll bet you must have wondered how it was I came to marry a cripple. It's a long story."

Her voice was as hypnotic as a tom-tom, and as monotonous. Already his mind and body were half asleep.

"It's a long, long story, and that's why I couldn't write it in a letter. I got into trouble when the Doyles lived above us on Center Street. I used to be kind to him and go to the movies with him because he was a cripple, although I was one of the most popular girls on the block. So when I got into trouble, I didn't know what to do and asked him for the money for an abortion. But he didn't have the money, so we got married instead. It all came through my trusting a dirty dago. I thought he was a gent, but when I ask him to marry me, why he spurned me from the door and wouldn't even give me money for an abortion. He said if he gave me the money that would mean it was his fault and I would have something on him. Did you ever hear of such a skunk?"

"No," he said. The life out of which she spoke was even heavier than her body. It was as if a gigantic, living Miss Lonelyhearts letter in the shape of a paper weight had been placed on his brain.

"After the baby was born, I wrote the skunk, but he never wrote back, and about two years ago, I got to thinking how unfair it was for Lucy to have to depend on a cripple and not come into her rights. So I looked his name up in the telephone book and took Lucy to see him. As I told him then, not that I wanted anything for myself, but just that I wanted Lucy to get what was coming to her. Well, after keeping us waiting in the hall over an hour—I was boiling mad, I can tell you, thinking of the wrong he had done me and my child—we were taken into the parlor by the butler. Very quiet and lady-like, because money ain't everything and he's no more a gent than I'm a lady, the dirty wop—I told him he ought to do something for Lucy see'n' he's her father. Well, he had the nerve to say that he had never seen me before and that if I didn't stop bothering him, he'd have me run in. That got me riled and I lit into the bastard and gave him a piece of my mind. A woman came in while we were arguing that I figured was his wife, so I hollered, 'He's the father of my child, he's the father of my child.' When they went to the 'phone to call a cop, I picked up the kid and beat it.

"And now comes the funniest part of the whole thing. My husband is a queer guy and he always makes believe that he is the father of the kid and even talks to me about *our* child. Well, when we got home, Lucy kept asking me why I said a strange man was her papa. She wanted to know if Doyle wasn't really her papa. I must of been crazy because I told her that she should remember that her real papa was a man named Tony Benelli and that he had wronged me. I told her a lot of other crap like that— too much movies I guess. Well, when Doyle got home the first thing Lucy says to him is that he ain't her papa. That got him sore and he wanted to know what I had told. I didn't like his high falutin' ways and said, 'The truth.' I guess too that I was kinda sick see'n him moon over her. He went for me and hit me on the cheek. I wouldn't let no man get away with that so I socked back and he swung at me with his stick but missed and fell on the floor and started to cry. The kid was on the floor crying too and that set me off because the next thing I know I'm on the floor bawling too."

She waited for him to comment, but he remained silent until she nudged him into speech with her elbow. "Your husband probably loves you and the kid," he said.

"Maybe so, but I was a pretty girl and could have had my pick. What girl wants to spend her life with a shrimp of a cripple?"

"You're still pretty," he said without knowing why, except that he was frightened.

She rewarded him with a kiss, then dragged him to the bed.

Miss Lonelyhearts

in the Dismal Swamp

SOON AFTER MRS. DOYLE LEFT, Miss Lonelyhearts became physically sick and was unable to leave his room. The first two days of his illness were blotted out by sleep, but on the third day, his imagination began again to work.

He found himself in the window of a pawnshop full of fur coats, diamond·rings, watches, shotguns, fishing tackle, mandolins. All these things were the paraphernalia of suffering. A tortured high light twisted on the blade of a gift knife, a battered horn grunted with pain.

He sat in the window thinking. Man has a tropism for order. Keys in one pocket, change in another. Mandolins are tuned G D A E. The physical world has a tropism for disorder, entropy. Man against Nature . . . the battle of the centuries. Keys yearn to mix with change. Mandolins strive to get out of tune.

Every order has within it the germ of destruction. All order is doomed, yet the battle is worth while.

A trumpet, marked to sell for $2.49, gave the call to battle and Miss Lonelyhearts plunged into the fray. First he formed a phallus of old watches and rubber boots, then a heart of umbrellas and trout flies, then a diamond of musical instruments and derby hats, after these a circle, triangle, square, swastika. But nothing proved definitive and he began to make a gigantic cross. When the cross became too large for the pawnshop, he moved it to the shore of the ocean. There every wave added to his stock faster than he could lengthen its arms. His labors were enormous. He staggered from the last wave line to his work, loaded down with marine refuse— bottles, shells, chunks of cork, fish heads, pieces of net.

Drunk with exhaustion, he finally fell asleep. When he awoke, he felt very weak, yet calm.

There was a timid knock on the door. It was open and Betty tiptoed into the room with her arms full of bundles. He made believe that he was asleep.

"Hello," he said suddenly.

Startled, she turned to explain. "I heard you were sick, so I brought some hot soup and other stuff."

He was too tired to be annoyed by her wide-eyed little mother act and let her feed him with a spoon. When he had finished eating, she opened the window and freshened the bed. As soon as the room was in order, she started to leave, but he called her back.

"Don't go, Betty."

She pulled a chair to the side of his bed and sat there without speaking.

"I'm sorry about what happened the other day," he said. "I guess I was sick."

She showed that she accepted his apology by helping him to excuse himself. "It's the Miss Lonelyhearts job. Why don't you give it up?"

"And do what?"

"Work in an advertising agency, or something."

"You don't understand, Betty, I can't quit. And even if I were to quit, it wouldn't make any difference. I wouldn't be able to forget the letters, no matter what I did."

"Maybe I don't understand," she said, "but I think you're making a fool of yourself."

"Perhaps I can make you understand. Let's start from the beginning. A man is hired to give advice to the readers of a newspaper. The job is a circulation stunt and the whole staff considers it a joke. He welcomes the job, for it might lead to a gossip column, and anyway he's tired of being a leg man. He too considers the job a joke, but after several months at it, the joke begins to escape him. He sees that the majority of the letters are profoundly humble pleas for moral and spiritual advice, that they are inarticulate expressions of genuine suffering. He also discovers that his correspondents take him seriously. For the first time in his life, he is forced to examine the values by which he lives. This examination shows him that he is the victim of the joke and not its perpetrator."

Although he had spoken soberly, he saw that Betty still thought him a fool. He closed his eyes.

"You're tired," she said. "I'll go."

"No, I'm not tired. I'm just tired of talking, you talk a while."

She told him about her childhood on a farm and of her love for animals about country sounds and country smells and of how fresh and clean everything in the country is. She said that he ought to live there and that if he did, he would find that all his troubles were city troubles.

While she was talking, Shrike burst into the room. He was drunk and immediately set up a great shout, as though he believed that Miss Lonelyhearts was too near death to hear distinctly. Betty left without saying good-by.

Shrike had evidently caught some of her farm talk, for he said: "My friend, I agree with Betty, you're an escapist. But I do not agree that the soil is the proper method for you to use."

Miss Lonelyhearts turned his face to the wall and pulled up the covers. But Shrike was unescapable. He raised his voice and talked through the blankets into the back of Miss Lonelyhearts' head.

"There are other methods, and for your edification I shall describe them. But first let us do the escape to the soil, as recommended by Betty:

"You are fed up with the city and its teeming millions. The ways and means of men, as getting and lending and spending, you lay waste your inner world, are too much with you. The bus takes too long, while the subway is always crowded. So what do you do? So you buy a farm and walk behind your horse's moist behind, no collar or tie, plowing your broad swift acres. As you turn up the rich black soil, the wind carries the smell of pine and dung across the fields and the rhythm of an old, old work enters your soul. To this rhythm, you sow and weep and chivy your kine, not kin or kind, between the pregnant rows of corn and taters. Your step becomes the heavy sexual step of a dance-drunk Indian and you tread the seed down into the female earth. You plant, not dragon's teeth, but beans and greens....

"Well, what do you say, my friend, shall it be the soil?"

Miss Lonelyhearts did not answer. He was thinking of how Shrike had accelerated his sickness by teaching him to handle his one escape, Christ, with a thick glove of words.

"I take your silence to mean that you have decided against the soil. I agree with you. Such a life is too dull and laborious. Let us now consider the South Seas:

"You live in a thatch hut with the daughter of the king, a slim young maiden in whose eyes is an ancient wisdom. Her breasts are golden speckled pears, her belly a melon, and her odor is like nothing so much as a jungle fern. In the evening, on the blue lagoon, under the silvery moon, to your love you croon in the soft sylabelew and vocabelew of her langorour tongorour. Your body is golden brown like hers, and tourists have need of the indignant finger of the missionary to point you out. They envy you your breech clout and carefree laugh and little brown bride and fingers instead of forks. But you don't return their envy, and when a beautiful society girl comes to your hut in the night, seeking to learn the secret of your happiness, you send her back to her yacht that hangs on the horizon like a nervous racehorse. And so you dream away the days, fishing, hunting, dancing, swimming, kissing, and picking flowers to twine in your hair. . . .

"Well, my friend, what do you think of the South Seas?"

Miss Lonelyhearts tried to stop him by making believe that he was asleep. But Shrike was not fooled.

"Again silence," he said, "and again you are right. The South Seas are played out and there's little use in imitating Gauguin. But don't be discouraged, we have only scratched the surface of our subject. Let us now examine Hedonism, or take the cash and let the credit go. . . .

"You dedicate your life to the pursuit of pleasure. No over-indulgence, mind you, but knowing that your body is a pleasure machine, you treat it carefully in order to get the most out of it. Golf as well as booze, Philadelphia Jack O'Brien and his chest-weights as well as Spanish dancers. Nor do you neglect the pleasures of the mind. You fornicate under pictures by Matisse and Picasso, you drink from Renaissance glassware, and often you spend an evening beside the fireplace with Proust and an apple. Alas, after much good fun, the day comes when you realize that soon you must die. You keep a stiff upper lip and decide to give a last party. You invite all your old mistresses, trainers, artists and boon companions. The guests are dressed in black, the waiters are coons, the table is a coffin carved for you by Eric Gill. You serve caviar and blackberries and licorice candy and coffee without cream. After the dancing girls have finished, you get to your feet and call for silence in order to explain your philosophy of life. 'Life,' you say, 'is a club where they won't stand for squawks, where they deal you only one hand and you must sit in. So even if the cards are cold and marked by the hand of fate, play up, play up like a gentleman and a sport. Get tanked, grab what's on the buffet, use the girls upstairs, but remember, when you throw box cars, take the curtain like a dead game sport, don't squawk.'. . .

"I won't even ask you what you think of such an escape. You haven't the money, nor are you stupid enough to manage it. But we come now to one that should suit you much better. . . .

"Art! Be an artist or a writer. When you are cold, warm yourself before the flaming tints of Titian, when you are hungry, nourish yourself with great spiritual foods by listening to the noble periods of Bach, the harmonies of Brahms and the thunder of Beethoven. Do you think there is anything in the fact that their names all begin with B? But don't take a chance, smoke a 3 B pipe, and remember these immortal lines: *When to the suddenness of melody the echo parting falls the failing day.* What a rhythm! Tell them to keep their society whores and pressed duck with oranges. For you *l'art vivant,* the living art, as you call it. Tell them that you know that your shoes are broken and that there are pimples on your face, yes, and that you have buck teeth and a club foot, but that you don't care, for to-morrow they are playing Beethoven's last quartets in Carnegie Hall and at home you have Shakespeare's plays in one volume."

After art, Shrike described suicide and drugs. When he had finished with them, he came to what he said was the goal of his lecture.

"My friend, I know of course that neither the soil, nor the South Seas, nor Hedonism, nor art, nor suicide, nor drugs, can mean anything to us. We are not men who swallow camels only to strain at stools. God alone is our escape. The church is our only hope, the First Church of Christ Dentist, where He is worshiped as Preventer of Decay. The church whose symbol is the trinity new-style: Father, Son and Wirehaired Fox Terrier.... And so, my good friend, let me dictate a letter to Christ for you:

Dear Miss Lonelyhearts of Miss Lonelyhearts—

I am twenty-six years old and in the newspaper game. Life for me is a desert empty of comfort. I cannot find pleasure in food, drink, or women—nor do the arts give me joy any longer. The Leopard of Discontent walks the streets of my city; the Lion of Discouragement crouches outside the walls of my citadel. All is desolation and a vexation of the spirit. I feel like hell. How can I believe, how can I have faith in this day and age? Is it true that the greatest scientists believe again in you?

I read your column and like it very much. There you once wrote: 'When the salt has

lost its savour, who shall savour it again?'
Is the answer: 'None but the Saviour?'
     Thanking you very much for a quick re-
ply, I remain yours truly,
                         A Regular Subscriber"

Miss Lonelyhearts

in the Country

BETTY CAME to see Miss Lonelyhearts the next day and every day thereafter. With her she brought soup and boiled chicken for him to eat.

He knew that she believed he did not want to get well, yet he followed her instructions because he realized that his present sickness was unimportant. It was merely a trick by his body to relieve one more profound.

Whenever he mentioned the letters or Christ, she changed the subject to tell long stories about life on a farm. She seemed to think that if he never talked about these things, his body would get well, that if his body got well everything would be well. He began to realize that there was a definite plan behind her farm talk, but could not guess what it was.

When the first day of spring arrived, he felt better. He had already spent more than a week in bed and was anxious to get out. Betty took him for a walk in the zoo and he was amused by her evident belief in the curative power of animals. She seemed to think that it must steady him to look at a buffalo.

He wanted to go back to work, but she made him get Shrike to extend his sick leave a few days. He was grateful to her and did as she asked. She then told him her plan. Her aunt still owned the farm in Connecticut on which she had been born and they could go there and camp in the house.

She borrowed an old Ford touring car from a friend. They loaded it with food and equipment and started out early one morning. As soon as they reached the outskirts of the city, Betty began to act like an excited child, greeting the trees and grass with delight.

After they had passed through New Haven, they came to Bramford and turned off the State highway on a dirt road that led to Monkstown. The road went through a wild-looking stretch of woods and they saw some red squirrels and a partridge. He had to admit, even to himself, that the pale new leaves, shaped and colored like candle flames, were beautiful and that the air smelt clean and alive.

There was a pond on the farm and they caught sight of it through the trees just before coming to the house. She did not have the key so they had to force the door open. The heavy, musty smell of old furniture and wood rot made them cough. He complained. Betty said that she did not mind because it was not a human smell. She put so much meaning into the word "human" that he laughed and kissed her.

They decided to camp in the kitchen because it was the largest room and the least crowded with old furniture. There were four windows and a door and they opened them all to air the place out.

While he unloaded the car, she swept up and made a fire in the stove out of a broken chair. The stove looked like a locomotive and was almost as large, but the chimney drew all right and she soon had a fire going. He got some water from the well and put it on the stove to boil. When the water was scalding hot, they used it to clean an old mattress that they had found in one of the bedrooms. Then they put the mattress out in the sun to dry.

It was almost sundown before Betty would let him stop working. He sat smoking a cigarette, while she prepared supper. They had beans, eggs, bread, fruit and drank two cups of coffee apiece.

After they had finished eating, there was still some light left and they went down to look at the pond. They sat close together with their backs against a big oak and watched a heron hunt frogs. Just as they were about to start back, two deer and a fawn came down to the water on the opposite side of the pond. The flies were bothering them and they went into the water and began to feed on the lily pads. Betty accidentally made a noise and the deer floundered back into the woods.

When they returned to the house, it was quite dark. They lit the kerosene lamp that they had brought with them, then dragged the mattress into the kitchen and made their bed on the floor next to the stove.

Before going to bed, they went out on the kitchen

porch to smoke a last cigarette. It was very cold and he had to go back for a blanket. They sat close together with the blanket wrapped around them.

There were plenty of stars. A screech owl made a horrible racket somewhere in the woods and when it quit, a loon began down on the pond. The crickets made almost as much noise as the loon.

Even with the blanket around them it was cold. They went inside and made a big fire in the stove, using pieces of a hardwood table to make the fire last. They each ate an apple, then put on their pajamas and went to bed. He fondled her, but when she said that she was a virgin, he let her alone and went to sleep.

He woke up with the sun in his eyes. Betty was already busy at the stove. She sent him down to the pond to wash and when he got back, breakfast was ready. It consisted of eggs, ham, potatoes, fried apples, bread and coffee.

After breakfast, she worked at making the place more comfortable and he drove to Monkstown for some fresh fruit and the newspapers. He stopped for gas at the Aw-Kum-On Garage and told the attendant about the deer. The man said that there was still plenty of deer at the pond because no yids ever went there. He said it wasn't the hunters who drove out the deer, but the yids.

He got back to the house in time for lunch and, after eating, they went for a walk in the woods. It was very sad under the trees. Although spring was well advanced, in the deep shade there was nothing but death—rotten leaves, gray and white fungi, and over everything a funereal hush.

Later it grew very hot and they decided to go for a swim. They went in naked. The water was so cold that they could only stay in for a short time. They ran back to the house and took a quick drink of gin, then sat in a sunny spot on the kitchen porch.

Betty was unable to sit still for long. There was nothing to do in the house, so she began to wash the underwear she had worn on the trip up. After she had finished, she rigged a line between two trees.

He sat on the porch and watched her work. She had her hair tied up in a checked handkerchief, otherwise she was completely naked. She looked a little fat, but when she lifted something to the line, all the fat disappeared. Her raised arms pulled her breasts up until they were like pink-tipped thumbs.

There was no wind to disturb the pull of the earth. The new green leaves hung straight down and shone in the hot sun like an army of little metal shields. Somewhere in the woods a thrush was singing. Its sound was like that of a flute choked with saliva.

Betty stopped with her arms high to listen to the bird. When it was quiet, she turned towards him with a guilty laugh. He blew her a kiss. She caught it with a gesture that was childishly sexual. He vaulted the porch rail and ran to kiss her. As they went down, he smelled a mixture of sweat, soap and crushed grass.

Miss Lonelyhearts

Returns

SEVERAL DAYS LATER, they started to drive back to the city. When they reached the Bronx slums, Miss Lonelyhearts knew that Betty had failed to cure him and that he had been right when he had said that he could never forget the letters. He felt better, knowing this, because he had begun to think himself a faker and a fool.

Crowds of people moved through the street with a dream-like violence. As he looked at their broken hands and torn mouths he was overwhelmed by the desire to help them, and because this desire was sincere, he was happy despite the feeling of guilt which accompanied it.

He saw a man who appeared to be on the verge of death stagger into a movie theater that was showing a picture called *Blonde Beauty*. He saw a ragged woman with an enormous goiter pick a love story magazine out of a garbage can and seem very excited by her find.

Prodded by his conscience, he began to generalize. Men have always fought their misery with dreams. Although dreams were once powerful, they have been made puerile by the movies, radio and newspapers. Among many betrayals, this one is the worst.

The thing that made his share in it particularly bad was that he was capable of dreaming the Christ dream. He felt that he had failed at it, not so much because of Shrike's jokes or his own self-doubt, but because of his lack of humility.

He finally got to bed. Before falling asleep, he vowed to make a sincere attempt to be humble. In the morning, when he started for his office, he renewed his vow.

Fortunately for him, Shrike was not in the city room and his humility was spared an immediate trial. He went straight to his desk and began to open letters. When he had opened about a dozen, he felt sick and decided to do his column for that day without reading any of them. He did not want to test himself too severely.

The typewriter was uncovered and he put a sheet of paper into the roller.

"Christ died for you.

"He died nailed to a tree for you. His gift to you is suffering and it is only through suffering that you can know Him. Cherish this gift for . . ."

He snatched the paper out of the machine. With him, even the word Christ was vanity. After staring at the pile of letters on his desk for a long time, he looked out the window. A slow spring rain was changing the dusty tar roofs below him to shiny patent leather. The water made everything slippery and he could find no support for either his eyes or his feelings.

Turning back to his desk, he picked up a bulky letter in a dirty envelope. He read it for the same reason that an animal tears at a wounded foot: to hurt the pain.

Dear Miss Lonelyhearts—

Being an admirer of your column because you give such good advice to people in trouble as that is what I am in also I would appreciate very much your advising me what to do after I tell you my troubles.

During the war I was told if I wanted to do my bit I should marry the man I was engaged to as he was going away to help Uncle Sam and to make a long story short I was married to him. After the war was over he still had to remain in the army for one more year as he signed for it and naturally I went to work as while doing this patriotic stunt he had only $18 dollars to his name. I worked for three years steady and then had to stay home because I became a mother and in the meantime of those years my husband would get a job and then would tire of it or want to roam. It was all right before the baby came because then I could work steady and then bills were paid but when I stopped everything went sliding backward.

Then two years went by and a baby boy was added to our union. My girl will be eight and my boy six years of age.

I made up my mind after I had the second child that in spite of my health as I was hit by an auto while carrying the first I would get some work to do but debts collected so rapidly it almost took a derick to lift them let alone a sick woman. I went to work evenings when my husband would be home so as somebody could watch the baby and I did this until the baby was three years old when I thought of taking in a man who had been boarding with his sister as she moved to Rochester and he had to look for a new place. Well my husband agreed as he figured the $15 dollars per he paid us would make it easier for him as this man was a widower with two children and as my husband knew him for twelve years being real pals then going out together etc. After the boarder was with us for about a year my husband didn't come home one night and then two nights etc. I listed him in the missing persons and after two and a half months I was told to go to Grove St. which I did and he was arrested because he refused to support me and my kids. When he served three months of the six the judge asked me to give him another chance which like a fool I did and when he got home he beat me up so I had to spend over $30 dollars in the dentist afterwards.

He got a pension from the army and naturally I was the one to take it to the store and cash it as he was so lazy I always had to sign his name and of course put per my name and through wanting to pay the landlord because he wanted to put us out I signed his check as usual but forgot to put per my name and for this to get even with me because he did three months time he sent to Washington for the copy of the check so I could be arrested for forgery but as the butcher knew about me signing the checks etc nothing was done to me.

He threatened my life many times saying no one solved the Mrs. Mills murder and the same will happen to you and many times when making beds I would find under his pillow a hammer, scissors, knife, stone lifter etc and when I asked him what the idea was he would make believe he knew nothing about it or say the children put them there and then a few months went by and I was going to my work as usual as the boarder had to stay home that day due to the fact the material for his boss did not arrive and he could not go to work as he is a piece worker. I always made a habit of setting the breakfast and cooking the food the night before so I could stay in bed until seven as at that time my son was in the Kings County hospital with a disease which my husband gave me that he got while fighting for Uncle Sam and I had to be at the clinic for the needle to. So while I was in bed unbeknown to me my husband sent the boarder out for a paper and when he came back my husband was gone. So later when I came from my room I was told that my husband had gone out. I fixed the childs breakfast and ate my own then went to the washtub to do the weeks wash and while the boarder was reading the paper at twelve o'clock noon my mother came over to mind the baby as I had a chance to go out and make a little money doing house work. Things were a little out of order beds not dressed and things out of place and a little sweeping had to be done as I was washing all morning and I didn't have a chance to do it so I thought to do it then while my mother was in the house with her to help me so that I could finish quickly. Hurrying at break neck speed to get finished I swept through the rooms to make sure everything was spick and span so when my husband came home he couldn't have anything to say. We had three beds and I was on the last which was a double bed when stooping to put the broom under the bed to get at the lint and the dust when lo and behold I saw a face like the mask of a devil with only the whites of the eyes showing and hands clenched to choke anyone and then I saw it move and I was so frighted that almost till night I was hystirical and I was paralised from my waist down. I thought I would never be able to walk again. A doctor was called for me by my mother and he said the man ought to be put in an asylum to do a thing like that. It was my husband lieing under the bed from seven in the morning until almost half past one o'clock lieing in his own dirt instead of going to the bath room when he had to be dirtied himself waiting to fright me.

So as I could not trust him I would not sleep with him and as I told the boarder to find a new place because I thought maybe he was jealous of something I slept in the boarders bed in an other room. Some nights I would wake up and find him standing by my bed laughing like a crazy man or walking around stripped etc.

I bought a new sowing machine as I do some sowing for other people to make both ends meet and one night while I was out delivering my work I got back to find the house cleaned out and he had pawned my sowing machine and also all the other pawnables in the house. Ever since he frighted me I have been so nervous during the night when I get up for the children that he would be standing behind a curtain and either jump out at me or put his hand on me before I could light the light. Well as I had to see that I could not make him work steady and that I had to be mother and housekeeper and wage earner etc and I could not let my nerves get the best of me as I lost a good job once on account of having bad nerves I simply moved away from him and anyway there was nothing much left in the house. But he pleaded with me for another chance so I thought seeing he is the father of my children I will and then he did more crazy things to many to write and I left him again. Four times we got together and four times I left. Please Miss Lonelyhearts believe me just for the childrens sake is the bunk and pardon me because I dont know how you are fixed but all I know is that in over three years I got $200 dollars from him altogether.

About four months ago I handed him a warrant for his arrest for non support and he tore it up and left the house and I haven't seen him since and as I had pneumonia and my girl had the flu I was put in financial embarasment with the doctor and we had to go to the ward and when we came out of the hospital I had to ask the boarder to come to live with us again as he was a sure $15 dollars a week and if anything happened to me he would be there to take care of the children. But he tries to make me be bad and as there is nobody in the house when he comes home drunk on Saturday night I dont know what to do but so far I didnt let him. Where my husband is I dont know but I received a vile letter from him where he even accused his inocent children of things and sarcastically asked about the star boarder.

Dear Miss Lonelyhearts please dont be angry at me for writing such a long letter

*and taking up so much of your time in read-
ing it but if I ever write all the things which
happened to me living with him it would fill
a book and please forgive me for saying some
nasty things as I had to give you an idea of
what is going on in my home. Every woman
is intitled to a home isnt she? So Miss Lonelyhearts please put a few lines in your column when you refer to this letter so I will
know you are helping me. Shall I take my
husband back? How can I support my children?*

*Thanking you for anything you can advise
me in I remain yours truly—*

Broad Shoulders

*P.S. Dear Miss Lonelyhearts dont think I
am broad shouldered but that is the way I
feel about life and me I mean.*

Miss Lonelyhearts

and the Cripple

MISS LONELYHEARTS dodged Betty because she made him feel ridiculous. He was still trying to cling to his humility, and the farther he got below self-laughter, the easier it was for him to practice it. When Betty telephoned, he refused to answer and after he had twice failed to call her back, she left him alone.

One day, about a week after he had returned from the country, Goldsmith asked him out for a drink. When he accepted, he made himself so humble that Goldsmith was frightened and almost suggested a doctor.

They found Shrike in Delehanty's and joined him at the bar. Goldsmith tried to whisper something to him about Miss Lonelyhearts' condition, but he was drunk and refused to listen. He caught only part of what Goldsmith was trying to say.

"I must differ with you, my good Goldsmith," Shrike said. "Don't call sick those who have faith. They are the well. It is you who are sick."

Goldsmith did not reply and Shrike turned to Miss Lonelyhearts. "Come, tell us, brother, how it was that you first came to believe. Was it music in a church, or the death of a loved one, or, mayhap, some wise old priest?"

The familiar jokes no longer had any effect on Miss Lonelyhearts. He smiled at Shrike as the saints are supposed to have smiled at those about to martyr them.

"Ah, but how stupid of me," Shrike continued. "It was the letters, of course. Did I myself not say that the Miss Lonelyhearts are the priests of twentieth-century America?"

Goldsmith laughed, and Shrike, in order to keep him laughing, used an old trick; he appeared to be offended. "Goldsmith, you are the nasty product of this unbelieving age. You cannot believe, you can only laugh. You take everything with a bag of salt and forget that salt is the enemy of fire as well as of ice. Be warned, the salt you use is not Attic salt, it is coarse butchers' salt. It doesn't preserve; it kills."

The bartender, who was standing close by, broke in to address Miss Lonelyhearts. "Pardon me, sir, but there's a gent here named Doyle who wants to meet you. He says you know his wife."

Before Miss Lonelyhearts could reply, he beckoned to someone standing at the other end of the bar. The signal was answered by a little cripple, who immediately started in their direction. He used a cane and dragged one of his feet behind him in a box-shaped shoe with a four-inch sole. As he hobbled along, he made many waste motions, like those of a partially destroyed insect.

The bartender introduced the cripple as Mr. Peter Doyle. Doyle was very excited and shook hands twice all around, then with a wave that was meant to be sporting, called for a round of drinks.

Before lifting his glass, Shrike carefully inspected the cripple. When he had finished, he winked at Miss Lonelyhearts and said, "Here's to humanity." He patted Doyle on the back. "Mankind, mankind . . ." he sighed, wagging his head sadly. "What is man that . . ."

The bartender broke in again on behalf of his friend and tried to change the conversation to familiar ground. "Mr. Doyle inspects meters for the gas company."

"And an excellent job it must be," Shrike said. "He should be able to give us the benefit of a different viewpoint. We newspapermen are limited in many ways and I like to hear both sides of a case."

Doyle had been staring at Miss Lonelyhearts as though searching for something, but he now turned to Shrike and tried to be agreeable. "You know what people say, Mr. Shrike?"

"No, my good man, what is it that people say?"

"Everybody's got a frigidaire nowadays, and they say that we meter inspectors take the place of the iceman in the stories." He tried, rather diffidently, to leer.

"What!" Shrike roared at him. "I can see, sir, that you are not the man for us. You can know nothing about humanity; you are humanity. I leave you to

Miss Lonelyhearts." He called to Goldsmith and stalked away.

The cripple was confused and angry. "Your friend is a nut," he said. Miss Lonelyhearts was still smiling, but the character of his smile had changed. It had become full of sympathy and a little sad.

The new smile was for Doyle and he knew it. He smiled back gratefully.

"Oh, I forgot," Doyle said, "the wife asked me, if I bumped into you, to ask you to our house to eat. That's why I made Jake introduce us."

Miss Lonelyhearts was busy with his smile and accepted without thinking of the evening he had spent with Mrs. Doyle. The cripple felt honored and shook hands for a third time. It was evidently his only social gesture.

After a few more drinks, when Doyle said that he was tired, Miss Lonelyhearts suggested that they go into the back room. They found a table and sat opposite each other.

The cripple had a very strange face. His eyes failed to balance; his mouth was not under his nose; his forehead was square and bony; and his round chin was like a forehead in miniature. He looked like one of those composite photographs' used by screen magazines in guessing contests.

They sat staring at each other until the strain of wordless communication began to excite them both. Doyle made vague, needless adjustments to his clothing. Miss Lonelyhearts found it very difficult to keep his smile steady.

When the cripple finally labored into speech, Miss Lonelyhearts was unable to understand him. He lis-

tened hard for a few minutes and realized that Doyle
was making no attempt to be understood. He was
giving birth to groups of words that lived inside of
him as things, a jumble of the retorts he had meant
to make when insulted and the private curses
against fate that experience had taught him to swallow.

Like a priest, Miss Lonelyhearts turned his face
slightly away. He watched the play of the cripple's
hands. At first they conveyed nothing but excitement, then gradually they became pictorial. They
lagged behind to illustrate a matter with which he
was already finished, or ran ahead to illustrate something he had not yet begun to talk about. As he grew
more articulate, his hands stopped trying to aid his
speech and began to dart in and out of his clothing
One of them suddenly emerged from a pocket of
his coat, dragging some sheets of letter paper. He
forced these on Miss Lonelyhearts.

Dear Miss Lonelyhearts—
I am kind of ashamed to write you because
a man like me dont take stock in things like
that but my wife told me you were a man
and not some dopey woman so I thought I
would write to you after reading your answer
to Disillusioned. I am a cripple 41 yrs of age
which I have been all my life and I have
never let myself get blue until lately when
I have been feeling lousy all the time on
account of not getting anywhere and asking
myself what is it all for. You have a educa-
tion so I figured may be you no. What I want

to no is why I go around pulling my leg up and down stairs reading meters for the gas company for a stinking $22.50 per while the bosses ride around in swell cars living off the fat of the land. Dont think I am a greasy red. I read where they shoot cripples in Russia because they cant work but I can work better than any park bum and support a wife and child to. But thats not what I am writing you about. What I want to no is what is it all for my pulling my god damned leg along the streets and down in stinking cellars with it all the time hurting fit to burst so that near quitting time I am crazy with pain and when I get home all I hear is money money which aint no home for a man like me. What I want to no is what in hell is the use day after day with a foot like mine when you have to go around pulling and scrambling for a lousy three squares with a toothache in it that comes from useing the foot so much. The doctor told me I ought to rest it for six months but who will pay me when I am resting it. But that aint what I mean either because you might tell me to change my job and where could I get another one I am lucky to have one at all. It aint the job that I am complaining about but what I want to no is what is the whole stinking business for.

Please write me an answer not in the paper because my wife reads your stuff and I dont want her to no I wrote to you because I

always said the papers is crap but I figured
maybe you no something about it because
you have read a lot of books and I never
even finished high.

> *Yours truly,*
> *Peter Doyle*

While Miss Lonelyhearts was puzzling out the crabbed writing, Doyle's damp hand accidently touched his under the table. He jerked away, but then drove his hand back and forced it to clasp the cripple's. After finishing the letter, he did not let go, but pressed it firmly with all the love he could manage. At first the cripple covered his embarrassment by disguising the meaning of the clasp with a handshake, but he soon gave in to it and they sat silently, hand in hand.

Miss Lonelyhearts

Pays a Visit

THEY LEFT THE SPEAKEASY TOGETHER, both very drunk and very busy: Doyle with the wrongs he had suffered and Miss Lonelyhearts with the triumphant thing that his humility had become.

They took a cab. As they entered the street in which Doyle lived, he began to curse his wife and his crippled foot. He called on Christ to blast them both.

Miss Lonelyhearts was very happy and inside of his head he was also calling on Christ. But his call was not a curse, it was the shape of his joy.

When the cab drew up to the curb, Miss Lonelyhearts helped his companion out and led him into the house. They made a great deal of noise with the front door and Mrs. Doyle came into the hall. At the sight of her the cripple started to curse again.

She greeted Miss Lonelyhearts, then took hold of

her husband and shook the breath out of him. When he was quiet, she dragged him into their apartment. Miss Lonelyhearts followed and as he passed her in the dark foyer, she goosed him and laughed.

After washing their hands, they sat down to eat. Mrs. Doyle had had her supper earlier in the evening and she waited on them. The first thing she put on the table was a quart bottle of guinea red.

When they had reached their coffee, she sat down next to Miss Lonelyhearts. He could feel her knee pressing his under the table, but he paid no attention to her and only broke his beatific smile to drink. The heavy food had dulled him and he was trying desperately to feel again what he had felt while holding hands with the cripple in the speakeasy.

She put her thigh under his, but when he still failed to respond, she got up abruptly and went into the parlor. They followed a few minutes later and found her mixing ginger-ale highballs.

They all drank silently. Doyle looked sleepy and his wife was just beginning to get drunk. Miss Lonelyhearts made no attempt to be sociable. He was busy trying to find a message. When he did speak it would have to be in the form of a message.

After the third highball, Mrs. Doyle began to wink quite openly at Miss Lonelyhearts, but he still refused to pay any attention to her. The cripple, however, was greatly disturbed by her signals. He began to fidget and mumble under his breath.

The vague noises he was making annoyed Mrs. Doyle. "What in hell are you talking about?" she demanded.

The cripple started a sigh that ended in a groan

and then, as though ashamed of himself, said, "Ain't I the pimp, to bring home a guy for my wife?" He darted a quick look at Miss Lonelyhearts and laughed apologetically.

Mrs. Doyle was furious. She rolled a newspaper into a club and struck her husband on the mouth with it. He surprised her by playing the fool. He growled like a dog and caught the paper in his teeth. When she let go of her end, he dropped to his hands and knees and continued the imitation on the floor.

Miss Lonelyhearts tried to get the cripple to stand up and bent to lift him; but as he did so, Doyle tore open Miss Lonelyhearts' fly, then rolled over on his back, laughing wildly.

His wife kicked him and turned away with a snort of contempt.

The cripple soon laughed himself out, and they all returned to their seats. Doyle and his wife sat staring at each other, while Miss Lonelyhearts again began to search for a message.

The silence bothered Mrs. Doyle. When she could stand it no longer, she went to the sideboard to make another round of drinks. But the bottle was empty. She asked her husband to go to the corner drug store for some gin. He refused with a single, curt nod of his head.

She tried to argue with him. He ignored her and she lost her temper. "Get some gin!" she yelled. "Get some gin, you bastard!"

Miss Lonelyhearts stood up. He had not yet found his message, but he had to say something. "Please don't fight," he pleaded. "He loves you, Mrs. Doyle; that's why he acts like that. Be kind to him."

She grunted with annoyance and left the room. They could hear her slamming things around in the kitchen.

Miss Lonelyhearts went over to the cripple and smiled at him with the same smile he had used in the speakeasy. The cripple returned the smile and stuck out his hand. Miss Lonelyhearts clasped it, and they stood this way, smiling and holding hands, until Mrs. Doyle reëntered the room.

"What a sweet pair of fairies you guys are," she said.

The cripple pulled his hand away and made as though to strike his wife. Miss Lonelyhearts realized that now was the time to give his message. It was now or never.

"You have a big, strong body, Mrs. Doyle. Holding your husband in your arms, you can warm him and give him life. You can take the chill out of his bones. He drags his days out in areaways and cellars, carrying a heavy load of weariness and pain. You can substitute a dream of yourself for this load. A buoyant dream that will be like a dynamo in him. You can do this by letting him conquer you in your bed. He will repay you by flowering and becoming ardent over you. . . ."

She was too astonished to laugh, and the cripple turned his face away as though embarrassed.

With the first few words Miss Lonelyhearts had known that he would be ridiculous. By avoiding God, he had failed to tap the force in his heart and had merely written a column for his paper.

He tried again by becoming hysterical. "Christ is love," he screamed at them. It was a stage scream, but he kept on. "Christ is the black fruit that hangs on the crosstree. Man was lost by eating of the forbidden fruit. He shall be saved by eating of the bidden fruit. The black Christ-fruit, the love fruit..."

This time he had failed still more miserably. He had substituted the rhetoric of Shrike for that of Miss Lonelyhearts. He felt like an empty bottle, shiny and sterile.

He closed his eyes. When he heard the cripple say, "I love you, I love you," he opened them and saw him kissing his wife. He knew that the cripple was doing this, not because of the things he had said, but out of loyalty.

"All right, you nut," she said, queening it over her husband. "I forgive you, but go to the drug store for some gin."

Without looking at Miss Lonelyhearts, the cripple took his hat and left. When he had gone Mrs. Doyle smiled. "You were a scream with your fly open," she said. "I thought I'd die laughing."

He did not answer.

"Boy, is he jealous," she went on. "All I have to do is point to some big guy and say, 'Gee, I'd love to have him love me up.' It drives him nuts."

Her voice was low and thick and it was plain that she was trying to excite him. When she went to the radio to tune in on a jazz orchestra, she waved her behind at him like a flag.

He said that he was too tired to dance. After doing a few obscene steps in front of him, she sat down in his lap. He tried to fend her off, but she kept pressing her open mouth against his and when he turned away, she nuzzled his cheek. He felt like an empty bottle that is being slowly filled with warm, dirty water.

When she opened the neck of her dress and tried to force his head between her breasts, he parted his knees with a quick jerk that spilled her to the floor. She tried to pull him down on top of her. He struck out blindly and hit her in the face. She screamed and he hit her again and again. He kept hitting her until she stopped trying to hold him, then he ran out of the house.

Miss Lonelyhearts

Attends a Party

Miss Lonelyhearts had gone to bed again. This time his bed was surely taking him somewhere, and with great speed. He had only to ride it quietly. He had already been riding for three days.

Before climbing aboard, he had prepared for the journey by jamming the telephone bell and purchasing several enormous cans of crackers. He now lay on the bed, eating crackers, drinking water and smoking cigarettes.

He thought of how calm he was. His calm was so perfect that he could not destroy it even by being conscious of it. In three days he had gone very far. It grew dark in the room. He got out of bed, washed his teeth, urinated, then turned out the light and went to sleep. He fell asleep without even a sigh and slept the sleep of the wise and the innocent. Without dreaming, he was aware of fireflies and the slop of oceans.

Later a train rolled into a station where he was a reclining statue holding a stopped clock, a coach rumbled into the yard of an inn where he was sitting over a guitar, cap in hand, shedding the rain with his hump.

He awoke. The noise of both arrivals had combined to become a knocking on the door. He climbed out of bed. Although he was completely naked, he went to the door without covering himself. Five people rushed in, two of whom were women. The women shrieked when they saw him and jumped back into the hall.

The three men held their ground. Miss Lonelyhearts recognized Shrike among them and saw that he as well as the others was very drunk. Shrike said that one of the women was his wife and wanted to fight Miss Lonelyhearts for insulting her.

Miss Lonelyhearts stood quietly in the center of the room. Shrike dashed against him, but fell back, as a wave that dashes against an ancient rock, smooth with experience, falls back. There was no second wave.

Instead Shrike became jovial. He slapped Miss Lonelyhearts on the back. "Put on a pair of pants, my friend," he said, "we're going to a party."

Miss Lonelyhearts picked up a can of crackers.

"Come on, my son," Shrike urged. "It's solitary drinking that makes drunkards."

Miss Lonelyhearts carefully examined each cracker before popping it into his mouth.

"Don't be a spoil-sport," Shrike said with a great

deal of irritation. He was a gull trying to lay an egg in the smooth flank of a rock, a screaming, clumsy gull. "There's a game we want to play and we need you to play it.—'Everyman his own Miss Lonely-hearts.' I invented it, and we can't play without you."

Shrike pulled a large batch of letters out of his pockets and waved them in front of Miss Lonely-hearts. He recognized them; they were from his office file.

The rock remained calm and solid. Although Miss Lonelyhearts did not doubt that it could withstand any test, he was willing to have it tried. He began to dress.

They went downstairs, and all six of them piled into one cab. Mary Shrike sat on his lap, but despite her drunken wriggling the rock remained perfect.

The party was in Shrike's apartment. A roar went up when Miss Lonelyhearts entered and the crowd surged forward. He stood firm and they slipped back in a futile curl. He smiled. He had turned more than a dozen drunkards. He had turned them without effort or thought. As he stood smiling, a little wave crept up out of the general welter and splashed at his feet for attention. It was Betty.

"What's the matter with you?" she asked. "Are you sick again?"

He did not answer.

When every one was seated, Shrike prepared to start the game. He distributed paper and pencils, then led Miss Lonelyhearts to the center of the room and began his spiel.

"Ladies and gentlemen," he said, imitating the voice and gestures of a circus barker. "We have with us tonight a man whom you all know and admire. Miss Lonelyhearts, he of the singing heart—a still more swollen Mussolini of the soul.

"He has come here to-night to help you with your moral and spiritual problems, to provide you with a slogan, a cause, an absolute value and a *raison d'être*.

"Some of you, perhaps, consider yourself too far gone for help. You are afraid that even Miss Lonelyhearts, no matter how fierce his torch, will be unable to set you on fire. You are afraid that even when exposed to his bright flame, you will only smolder and give off a bad smell. Be of good heart, for I know that you will burst into flame. Miss Lonelyhearts is sure to prevail."

Shrike pulled out the batch of letters and waved them above his head.

"We will proceed systematically," he said. "First, each of you will do his best to answer one of these letters, then, from your answers, Miss Lonelyhearts will diagnose your moral ills. Afterwards he will lead you in the way of attainment."

Shrike went among his guests and distributed the letters as a magician does cards. He talked continuously and read a part of each letter before giving it away.

"Here's one from an old woman whose son died last week. She is seventy years old and sells pencils for a living. She has no stockings and wears heavy boots on her torn and bleeding feet. She has rheum in her eyes. Have you room in your heart for her?

"This one is a jim-dandy. A young boy wants a violin. It looks simple; all you have to do is get the kid one. But then you discover that he has dictated the letter to his little sister. He is paralyzed and can't even feed himself. He has a toy violin and hugs it to his chest, imitating the sound of playing with his mouth. How pathetic! However, one can learn much from this parable. Label the boy Labor, the violin Capital, and so on . . ."

Miss Lonelyhearts stood it with the utmost serenity; he was not even interested. What goes on in the sea is of no interest to the rock.

When all the letters had been distributed, Shrike gave one to Miss Lonelyhearts. He took it, but after holding it for a while, he dropped it to the floor without reading it.

Shrike was not quiet for a second.

"You are plunging into a world of misery and suffering, peopled by creatures who are strangers to everything but disease and policemen. Harried by one, they are hurried by the other. . . .

"Pain, pain, pain, the dull, sordid, gnawing, chronic pain of heart and brain. The pain that only a great spiritual liniment can relieve. . . ."

When Miss Lonelyhearts saw Betty get up to go, he followed her out of the apartment. She too should see the rock he had become.

Shrike did not miss him until he discovered the letter on the floor. He picked it up, tried to find Miss Lonelyhearts, then addressed the gathering again.

"The master has disappeared," he announced, "but do not despair. I am still with you. I am his disciple and I shall lead you in the way of attainment. First let me read you this letter which is addressed directly to the master."

He took the letter out of its envelope, as though he had not read it previously, and began: " 'What kind of a dirty skunk are you? When I got home with the gin, I found my wife crying on the floor and the house full of neighbors. She said that you tried to rape her you dirty skunk and they wanted to get the police but I said that I'd do the job myself you . . .'

"My, oh my, I really can't bring myself to utter such vile language. I'll skip the swearing and go on. 'So that's what all your fine speeches come to, you bastard, you ought to have your brains blown out.' It's signed, 'Doyle.'

"Well, well, so the master is another Rasputin. How this shakes one's faith! But I can't believe it. I won't believe it. The master can do no wrong. My faith is unshaken. This is only one more attempt against him by the devil. He has spent his life struggling with the arch fiend for our sakes, and he shall triumph. I mean Miss Lonelyhearts, not the devil.

"The gospel according to Shrike. Let me tell you about his life. It unrolls before me like a scroll. First, in the dawn of childhood, radiant with pure innocence, like a rain-washed star, he wends his weary way to the University of Hard Knocks. Next, a youth, he dashes into the night from the bed of his first whore. And then, the man, the man Miss Lonelyhearts struggling valiantly to realize a high ideal, his course shaped by a proud aim. But, alas! cold and scornful the world heaps obstacle after obstacle in his path; deems he the goal at hand, a voice of thunder bids him 'Halt!' 'Let each hindrance be thy ladder,' thinks he. 'Higher, even higher, mount!' And so he climbs, rung by weary rung, and so he urges himself on, breathless with hallowed fire. And so . . ."

Miss Lonelyhearts

and the Party Dress

WHEN MISS LONELYHEARTS left Shrike's apartment, he found Betty in the hall waiting for the elevator. She had on a light-blue dress that was very much a party dress. She dressed for things, he realized.

Even the rock was touched by this realization. No; it was not the rock that was touched. The rock was still perfect. It was his mind that was touched, the instrument with which he knew the rock.

He approached Betty with a smile, for his mind was free and clear. The things that muddied it had precipitated out into the rock.

But she did not smile back. "What are you grinning at?" she snapped.

"Oh, I'm sorry," he said. "I didn't mean anything."

They entered the elevator together. When they

reached the street, he took her arm although she tried to jerk away.

"Won't you have a soda, please?" he begged. The party dress had given his simplified mind its cue and he delighted in the boy-and-girl argument that followed.

"No; I'm going home."

"Oh, come on," he said, pulling her towards a soda fountain. As she went, she unconsciously exaggerated her little-girl-in-a-party-dress air.

They both had strawberry sodas. They sucked the pink drops up through straws, she pouting at his smile, neither one of them conscious of being cute.

"Why are you mad at me, Betty? I didn't do anything. It was Shrike's idea and he did all the talking."

"Because you are a fool."

"I've quit the Miss Lonelyhearts job. I haven't been in the office for almost a week."

"What are you going to do?"

"I'm going to look for a job in an advertising agency."

He was not deliberately lying. He was only trying to say what she wanted to hear. The party dress was so gay and charming, light blue with a frothy lace collar flecked with pink, like the collar of her soda.

"You ought to see Bill Wheelright about a job. He owns an agency—he's a swell guy.... He's in love with me."

"I couldn't work for a rival."

She screwed up her nose and they both laughed. He was still laughing when he noticed that something had gone wrong with her laugh. She was crying.

He felt for the rock. It was still there; neither laughter nor tears could affect the rock. It was oblivious to wind or rain.

"Oh..." she sobbed. "I'm a fool." She ran out of the store.

He followed and caught her. But her sobs grew worse and he hailed a taxi and forced her to get in.

She began to talk under her sobs. She was pregnant. She was going to have a baby.

He put the rock forward and waited with complete poise for her to stop crying. When she was quiet, he asked her to marry him.

"No," she said. "I'm going to have an abortion."

"Please marry me." He pleaded just as he had pleaded with her to have a soda.

He begged the party dress to marry him, saying all the things it expected to hear, all the things that went with strawberry sodas and farms in Connecticut. He was just what the party dress wanted him to be: simple and sweet, whimsical and poetic, a trifle collegiate yet very masculine.

By the time they arrived at her house, they were discussing their life after marriage. Where they would live and in how many rooms. Whether they could afford to have the child. How they would rehabilitate the farm in Connecticut. What kind of furniture they both liked.

She agreed to have the child. He won that point. In return, he agreed to see Bill Wheelright about a job. With a great deal of laughter, they decided to have three beds in their bedroom. Twin beds for sleep, very prim and puritanical, and between them a love bed, an ornate double bed with cupids, nymphs and Pans.

He did not feel guilty. He did not feel. The rock was a solidification of his feeling, his conscience, his sense of reality, his self-knowledge. He could have planned anything. A castle in Spain and love on a balcony or a pirate trip and love on a tropical island.

When her door closed behind him, he smiled. The rock had been thoroughly tested and had been found perfect. He had only to climb aboard the bed again.

Miss Lonelyhearts Has

a Religious Experience

AFTER A LONG NIGHT and morning, towards noon, Miss Lonelyhearts welcomed the arrival of fever. It promised heat and mentally unmotivated violence. The promise was soon fulfilled; the rock became a furnace.

He fastened his eyes on the Christ that hung on the wall opposite his bed. As he stared at it, it became a bright fly, spinning with quick grace on a background of blood velvet sprinkled with tiny nerve stars.

Everything else in the room was dead—chairs, table, pencils, clothes, books. He thought of this black world of things as a fish. And he was right, for it suddenly rose to the bright bait on the wall. It rose with a splash of music and he saw its shining silver belly.

Christ is life and light.

"Christ! Christ!" This shout echoed through the innermost cells of his body.

He moved his head to a cooler spot on the pillow and the vein in his forehead became less swollen. He felt clean and fresh. His heart was a rose and in his skull another rose bloomed.

The room was full of grace. A sweet, clean grace, not washed clean, but clean as the innersides of the inner petals of a newly forced rosebud.

Delight was also in the room. It was like a gentle wind, and his nerves rippled under it like small blue flowers in a pasture.

He was conscious of two rhythms that were slowly becoming one. When they became one, his identification with God was complete. His heart was the one heart, the heart of God. And his brain was likewise God's.

God said, "Will you accept it, now?"

And he replied, "I accept, I accept."

He immediately began to plan a new life and his future conduct as Miss Lonelyhearts. He submitted drafts of his column to God and God approved them. God approved his every thought.

Suddenly the door bell rang. He climbed out of bed and went into the hall to see who was coming. It was Doyle, the cripple, and he was slowly working his way up the stairs.

God had sent him so that Miss Lonelyhearts could perform a miracle and be certain of his conversion. It was a sign. He would embrace the cripple and the cripple would be made whole again, even as he, a spiritual cripple, had been made whole.

He rushed down the stairs to meet Doyle with his arms spread for the miracle.

Doyle was carrying something wrapped in a newspaper. When he saw Miss Lonelyhearts, he put his hand inside the package and stopped. He shouted some kind of a warning, but Miss Lonelyhearts continued his charge. He did not understand the cripple's shout and heard it as a cry for help from Desperate, Harold S., Catholic-mother, Brokenhearted, Broad-shoulders, Sick-of-it-all, Disillusioned-with-tubercular-husband. He was running to succor them with love.

The cripple turned to escape, but he was too slow and Miss Lonelyhearts caught him.

While they were struggling, Betty came in through the street door. She called to them to stop and started up the stairs. The cripple saw her cutting off his escape and tried to get rid of the package. He pulled his hand out. The gun inside the package exploded and Miss Lonelyhearts fell, dragging the cripple with him. They both rolled part of the way down the stairs.

AFTERWORD

NATHANAEL WEST was born Nathan Weinstein in New York City on October 17, 1903, the child of Jewish immigrants from Russia. His mother, Anna Wallenstein Weinstein, came of a cultivated family, and had been a beautiful girl, courted in Europe by the painter Maurice Stern. As a housewife she turned stout and bossy. West's father, Max Weinstein, a building contractor, was slight, kind, and shy. Of West's two sisters, the elder, Hinda, somewhat resembled the mother, and the younger, Lorrain (called Laura), was more like the father. West was particularly devoted to his father, and so close to his younger sister that in later life he repeatedly said he could never marry less fine a woman than his sister Laura.

The boy West attended P.S. 81 and P.S. 10, both in Manhattan, where he showed no academic distinc-

tion. He was a thin, awkward, and ungainly child.
Summers he went to Camp Paradox in the Adirondacks, and a former counselor remembers him as "a
quiet chap and not much of a mixer." Baseball was
his passion, although he tended to daydream in the
outfield. When a fly ball hit him on the head and
bounced off for a home run, he got the nickname,
"Pep," that stayed with him all his life.

Otherwise West seems to have spent most of his
time reading. If his sisters' recollection can be trust-
ed, he read Tolstoi at ten, and by thirteen he was
familiar with Dostoevski and other Russian literature, Flaubert, and Henry James. He trained his bull
terrier to bite anyone who came into his room when
he was reading. After his graduation from P.S. 10,
West enrolled at De Witt Clinton High School,
where he soon distinguished himself as one of the
weakest students in the school. He took no part in
any extracurricular activity. In June 1920, West left
Clinton without graduating.

In September 1921, West was admitted to Tufts
University, on the strength of what now seems to
have been a forged transcript from De Witt Clinton.
Two months later, as a result of academic difficulties,
he withdrew. In February 1922, he was admitted to
Brown University as a transfer student from Tufts,
this time on the basis of the transcript of the record
of another Nathan Weinstein at Tufts. Once enrolled at Brown, West got serious, and managed not
only to pass his courses but to graduate in two and
a half years.

At Brown, West developed another personality,
or showed another side of his personality than the

solitary dreamer. He became an Ivy League fashion plate, wearing Brooks Brothers suits and shirts, and a homburg. A college friend, Jeremiah Mahoney, recalls that West looked like a "well-heeled mortuary assistant." Although his manner was reserved, he was friendly and gregarious, generous with his large allowance from his father, and a fairly good banjo player. With girls, he tended to be either too shy or too brash. One summer, West and another college friend, Quentin Reynolds, worked as hod carriers for West's father, and West not only built muscles on his thin frame but got on surprisingly well with the workmen.

West received little or no education in the Jewish religion, and although he was probably ritually circumcised, he was never confirmed in a Bar Mitzvah ceremony. During his years at Brown, West threw off what he could of his Jewishness, and suffered from the rest. "More than anyone I ever knew," his friend John Sanford later reported, "Pep writhed under the accidental curse of his religion." West had nothing to do with any organized Jewish activity on campus, hung around the snobbish Gentile fraternities, and was intensely anxious to be pledged and intensely bitter that he never was. "Nobody ever thought of Pep as being Jewish," a college friend has said, but apparently the Brown fraternities did.

West's great success at Brown was as an aesthete. He dabbled in mysticism, ritual magic, and medieval Catholicism, quoted from obscure saints, discovered Joyce, and for a while was a Nietzschean. S. J. Perelman, a college friend who later married West's sister Laura, recalls that West was the first man on campus to read *Jurgen.* He was equally devoted to Baudelaire, Verlaine, Rimbaud, Huysmans and Arthur Machen. His personal library was the largest any Brown man had at the time, and he loaned books liberally. Relying on the other Nathan Weinstein's credits in science and economics, West was able to confine himself almost entirely to courses in literature, philosophy, and history. His principal extracurricular activity was working as an editor of *Casements,* the Brown literary magazine. He drew its first cover design, naturally of casements, and contributed a poem, "Death," and an article, "Euripides—a Playwright." The 1924 *Liber Brunensis,* the yearbook, identified West as a genius with an unpredictable future.

After his graduation in 1924, West persuaded his father to send him to Paris, where he spent two happy years and grew a red beard. He returned to New York early in 1926, worked for his father for a while, and then in 1927, through a family connection, got a job as assistant manager at the Kenmore Hotel on East 23rd Street. Put on night duty, he was able to spend the nights reading. He gave rooms to his Brown friends and *their* homeless friends, among them Dashiell Hammett, who finished *The Maltese Falcon* as West's bootleg guest at the Kenmore. In 1928 he progressed to the same job at a fancier hotel, the Sutton on East 56th Street, where he put up other indigent writers, at reduced rates or no charge at all, among them Erskine Caldwell and James T. Farrell. After the stock market crash, which ruined West's father, the Sutton's sun deck became

a favorite spot for suicides, and West took to calling
it "Suicide Leap."

West's first novel, *The Dream Life of Balso Snell*,
seems to have been first written in college, but he
rewrote it at the Sutton, and in 1931 he managed to
get it privately printed in a limited edition of 500
copies. One review appeared, in *Contempo*, but
otherwise *Balso Snell* caused no stir whatsoever. The
book listed "Nathanael West" as author and thus
marked West's official change of name. He had
spent much of his class time at Brown doodling
"Nathan von Wallenstein Weinstein," which was the
name signed to his *Casements* contributions, but
even that had turned out to be not Gentile enough.
West explained to William Carlos Williams how he
got the name: "Horace Greeley said, 'Go West,
young man.' So I did." West's anti-Semitism was now
considerable. He referred to Jewish girls as "bagels,"
and avoided them.

In 1931, West took a leave from the Sutton and
he and Sanford, another aspiring novelist, rented a
shack in the Adirondacks near Warrensburg, New
York. Here they wrote in the mornings and fished
and hunted in the afternoons. West was working on
Miss Lonelyhearts, reading each sentence back
aloud, producing about a hundred words a day. He
rewrote the manuscript five or six times, in the
Adirondacks, then back at the Sutton; finally, having
quit the Sutton, in a hotel in Frenchtown, New
Jersey.

Late in 1932 West and the Perelmans bought a
farmhouse in Bucks County, Pennsylvania, and Mrs.
Weinstein soon moved in to take over the cooking

and try to persuade West to return to the hotel business. In 1933 *Miss Lonelyhearts* was published, and it was reviewed enthusiastically. Unfortunately, the publisher, Horace Liveright, chose that moment to go bankrupt, the printer refused to deliver most of the edition, and by the time West got another publisher to take it over, the reviews were forgotten. Altogether *Miss Lonelyhearts* sold fewer than 800 copies, and West's total income from his first two books and three years of writing came to $780.

In 1932 West had become co-editor with Dr. Williams of a little magazine, *Contact,* and he published articles and chapters of *Miss Lonelyhearts* in it and in *Contempo* in 1933. In August 1933, he became associate editor of a magazine, *Americana,* edited by Alexander King. Before *Americana* expired in November, West managed to publish a Hollywood story, "Business Deal," and some excerpts from *Balso Snell* in it. West then wrote some stories for the slick magazines, but did not succeed in selling any. He applied for a Guggenheim fellowship, with F. Scott Fitzgerald as one of his sponsors, but failed to get it.

West next wrote *A Cool Million* in a hurry, hoping to profit from the reviews of *Miss Lonelyhearts* and make some money. It appeared in 1934, was unfavorably reviewed, sold poorly, and was soon remaindered.

West's personal life in the East was no more successful than his literary career. *Balso Snell* was dedicated to Alice Shepard, a Roman Catholic girl who had gone to Pembroke College with West's sister Laura. He was secretly engaged to her from 1929 to 1932, then publicly engaged, but they never married, although West had bought a marriage license and carried it around with him for several years. His poverty was the explanation given out, but in Sanford's opinion the engagement foundered on the religious difference.

West had been to Hollywood for a few months in 1933, when *Miss Lonelyhearts* was sold to Twentieth Century-Fox and West received a writing contract at $350 a week. He was given little to do, saw his novel made into a Lee Tracy murder thriller, and came back to New York in July disillusioned and bitter. Nevertheless, in 1935, when every other possibility seemed closed to him, West returned to Hollywood and went to work for Republic Studios as a script writer. He switched to RKO Radio in 1938, and also worked for Universal-International Pictures. In the remaining few years of his life, West turned out a number of trivial screenplays, alone or in collaboration, among them *Five Came Back*, *I Stole a Million*, and *Spirit of Culver*. As a result of his facility as a script writer, West was able to live in comfort and security for the first time since the 1929 crash. He worked a few hours a week dictating to a secretary, and spent most of his weekends on hunting trips, following the season down from Oregon through California into Mexico each year. He acquired two hunting dogs, which slept on his bed, and he explained to people that he needed a house and servants for the dogs.

West made it clear that he despised the "pants pressers" of Hollywood, and he tried to escape in a number of fashions. He collaborated on two plays for Broadway, but the first never got there and the second only lasted two performances, winning from Brooks Atkinson the accolade "nitwit theatre." He became a fellow traveler of the Communist party, signing the call for the American Writers Congress in 1935, joining the Screen Writers Guild, and working strenuously on behalf of Loyalist Spain and other causes. (Earlier, in 1933, he had published a Marxist poem in *Contempo*. Before leaving for California in 1935 he had picketed Ohrbach's with other Communist sympathizers and was jailed for a few hours "for obstructing traffic.") He was, luckily, unable to get his political orientation explicitly into his fiction.

West published *The Day of the Locust* in 1939, hoping its success would get him out of Hollywood, but despite some good reviews it was a commercial failure, selling fewer than 1500 copies. (West's publisher, Bennett Cerf, explained to him that it failed because women readers didn't like it.)

West's isolation ended suddenly and surprisingly in 1940, when he fell in love with Eileen McKenney, the protagonist of Ruth McKenney's *My Sister Eileen*. They were married in April, and spent a three-month honeymoon in Oregon, hunting and fishing. On West's return he got a higher paid job at Columbia Pictures; later Columbia bought *A Cool Million* and a screen treatment of it on which West had collaborated. The great happy period of West's life, begun in the spring, did not last out the year. On December 22, the Wests were returning from a hunting trip in Mexico, when West, a poor driver, went through a stop sign near El Centro, California. Their station wagon crashed into an automobile. Eileen died instantly. West an hour later on the way to the hospital. He was thirty-seven. His body was shipped to New York and buried in a Jewish cemetery.

Since his death West's reputation has risen continuously. *Miss Lonelyhearts* has sold 190,000 copies in paperback, and *The Day of the Locust* 250,000. Scholarly articles about West, here and abroad, multiply cancerously. *Miss Lonelyhearts* has been made into a play, a more faithful film than the Lee Tracy one, and an opera. In 1946 it was translated into French by Marcelle Sibon as *Mademoiselle Cœur-Brisé*, with an introduction by Philippe Soupault, and it has had a visible effect on later French fiction. Since 1949, all West's books but the first have been published in England. When the four novels were reissued in this country in one volume in 1957, all the reviews were favorable, and there was general agreement that West was one of the most important writers of the thirties, as American as apple pie. West's picture appeared on the cover of the *Saturday Review*, looking very Jewish.

Far and away the best of West's books, and in my opinion the only one assured of permanent survival, is *Miss Lonelyhearts*. No one who read West's first book, *The Dream Life of Balso Snell*, a juvenile and somewhat tiresome production, in 1931, could have expected the assured mastery of *Miss Lonelyhearts* two years later, in 1933. In an interview at the time West told A. J. Liebling that it was entirely unlike *Balso Snell*, "of quite a different make, wholesome, clean, holy, slightly mystic and inane." He describes it in an article "Some Notes on Miss Lonelyhearts," as a "portrait of a priest of our time who has had a religious experience." In it, West explains, "violent images are used to illustrate commonplace events. Violent acts are left almost bald." He credits Willam James's *Varieties of Religious Experience* for its psychology. Some or all of this may be Westian leg-pull.

The plot of *Miss Lonelyhearts* is Sophoclean irony, as simple and inevitable as the plot of *Balso Snell* is random and whimsical. A young newspaperman who writes the agony column of his paper as "Miss Lonelyhearts" has reached the point where the joke has gone sour. He becomes obsessed with the real misery of his correspondents, illuminated for him by the cynicism of William Shrike, the feature editor. Miss Lonelyhearts pursues Shrike's wife Mary, un-successfully, and cannot content himself with the love and radiant goodness of Betty, his fiancée. Eventually he finds his fate in two of his correspond-ents, the crippled Peter Doyle and his wife Fay. Miss Lonelyhearts is not punished for his tumble with Fay, but when on his next encounter he fights her off, it leads to his being shot by Doyle.

The characters are allegorical figures who are at the same time convincing as people. Miss Lonely-hearts is a New England puritan, the son of a Baptist minister. He has a true religious vocation or calling, but no institutional church to embody it. When Betty suggests that he quit the column, he tells her: "I can't quit. And even if I were to quit, it wouldn't make any difference. I wouldn't be able to forget the letters, no matter what I did."

In one of the most brilliant strokes in the book, he is never named, always identified only by his role.

(In an earlier draft, West had named him Thomas Matlock, which we could translate "Doubter Wrestler," but no name at all is infinitely more effective.) Even when he telephones Fay Doyle for an assignation, he identifies himself only as "Miss Lonelyhearts, the man who does the column." In his namelessness, in his vocation without a church, Miss Lonelyhearts is clearly the prophet in the reluctance stage, when he denies the call and tells God that he stammers, but Miss Lonelyhearts, the prophet of *our* time, is stuck there until death.

Miss Lonelyhearts identifies Betty as the principle of order: "She had often made him feel that when she straightened his tie, she straightened much more." The order that she represents is the innocent order of Nature, as opposed to the disorder of sinful Man. When Miss Lonelyhearts is sick, Betty comes to nourish him with hot soup, impose order on his room, and redeem him with a pastoral vision: "She told him about her childhood on a farm and of her love for animals, about country sounds and country smells and of how fresh and clean everything in the country is. She said that he ought to live there and that if he did, he would find that all his troubles were city troubles." When Miss Lonelyhearts is back on his feet, Betty takes him for a walk in the zoo, and he is "amused by her evident belief in the curative power of animals." Then she takes him to live in the country for a few days, in the book's great idyllic scene. Miss Lonelyhearts is beyond help, but it is Betty's patient innocence—she is as soft and helpless as a kitten—that makes the book so heartbreaking. She is an innocent Eve to his fallen Adam, and he alone is driven out of Eden.

The book's four other principal characters are savage caricatures, in the root sense of "caricature" as the overloading of one attribute. Shrike is a dissociated half of Miss Lonelyhearts, his cynical intelligence, and it is interesting to learn that Shrike's rhetorical masterpiece, the great speech on the varieties of escape, was spoken by Miss Lonelyhearts in an earlier draft. Shrike's name is marvelously apt. The shrike or butcherbird impales its prey on thorns, and the name is a form of the word "shriek." Shrike is of course the mocker who hands Miss Lonelyhearts his crown of thorns, and throughout the book he is a shrieking bird of prey; when not a butcherbird, "a screaming, clumsy gull."

Shrike's wife Mary is one vast teasing mammary image. As Miss Lonelyhearts decides to telephone Mary in Delehanty's speakeasy, he sees a White Rock poster and observes that "the artist had taken a great deal of care in drawing her breasts and their nipples stuck out like tiny red hats." He then thinks of "the play Mary made with her breasts. She used them as the coquettes of long ago had used their fans. One of her tricks was to wear a medal low down on her chest. Whenever he asked to see it, instead of drawing it out she leaned over for him to look. Although he had often asked to see the medal, he had not yet found out what it represented." Miss Lonelyhearts and Mary go out for a gay evening, and Mary flaunts her breasts while talking of her mother's terrible death from cancer of the breast. He finally gets to see the medal, which reads "Awarded by the Boston Latin School for first place in the

100 yd. dash." When he takes her home he kisses her breasts, for the first time briefly slowing down her dash.

The Doyles are presented in inhuman or subhuman imagery. When, in answer to Fay's letter of sexual invitation, Miss Lonelyhearts decides to telephone her, he pictures her as "a tent, hair-covered and veined," and himself as a skeleton: "When he made the skeleton enter the flesh tent, it flowered at every joint." Fay appears and is a giant: "legs like Indian clubs, breasts like balloons and a brow like a pigeon." When he takes her arm, "It felt like a thigh." Following her up the stairs to his apartment, "he watched the action of her massive hams; they were like two enormous grindstones." Undressing, "she made sea sounds; something flapping like a sail; there was the creak of ropes; then he heard the wave-against-a-wharf smack of rubber on flesh. Her call for him to hurry was a sea-moan, and when he lay beside her, she heaved, tidal, moon-driven." Eventually Miss Lonelyhearts "crawled out of bed like an exhausted swimmer leaving the surf," and she soon drags him back.

If Fay is an oceanic monster, Peter Doyle is only a sinister puppy. In bringing Miss Lonelyhearts back to the apartment at Fay's order, he half-jokes, "Ain't I the pimp, to bring home a guy for my wife?" Fay reacts by hitting him in the mouth with a rolled-up newspaper, and his comic response is to growl like a dog and catch the paper with his teeth. When she lets go of her end he drops to his hands and knees and continues to imitate a dog on the floor. As Miss Lonelyhearts leans over to help him up, "Doyle tore open Miss Lonelyhearts' fly, then rolled over on his back, laughing wildly." Fay, more properly, accepts him as a dog and kicks him.

The obsessive theme of *Miss Lonelyhearts* is human pain and suffering, but it is represented almost entirely as female suffering. This is first spelled out in the letters addressed to Miss Lonelyhearts: Sick-of-it-all is a Roman Catholic wife who has had seven children in twelve years, is pregnant again, and has kidney pains so excruciating that she cries all the time. Desperate is a sixteen-year-old born with a hole in her face instead of a nose, who wants to have dates like other girls. Harold S. writes about his thirteen-year-old deaf-and-dumb sister Gracie, who was raped by a man when she was playing on the roof, and who will be brutally punished if her parents find out about it. Broad Shoulders was hit by a car when she was first pregnant, and is alternately persecuted and deserted by an unbalanced husband, in five pages of ghastly detail. Miss Lonelyhearts gets only two letters about male suffering, one from a paralyzed boy who wants to play the violin, the other from Peter Doyle, who complains of the pain from his crippled leg and the general meaninglessness of life.

The theme of indignities committed on women comes up in another form in the stories Miss Lonelyheart's friends tell in Delehanty's. They seem to be exclusively anecdotes of group rape, of one woman gang-raped by eight neighbors, of another kept in the back room of a speakeasy for three days, until "on the last day they sold tickets to niggers." Miss Lonelyhearts identifies himself with "wife-torturers, rapers of small children." At one point he tries giving his readers the traditional Christian justification for suffering, that it is Christ's gift to mankind to bring them to Him, but he tears up the column.

Ultimately the novel cannot justify or even explain suffering, only proclaim its omnipresence. Lying sick in bed, Miss Lonelyhearts gets a vision of human life: "He found himself in the window of a pawnshop full of fur coats, diamond rings, watches, shotguns, fishing tackle, mandolins. All these things were the paraphernalia of suffering. A tortured high light twisted on the blade of a gift knife, a battered horn grunted with pain." Finally his mind forms everything into a gigantic cross, and he falls asleep exhausted.

The book's desperate cry of pain and suffering comes to a focus in what Miss Lonelyhearts calls his "Christ complex." He recognizes that Christ is the only answer to his readers' letters, but that "if he did not want to get sick, he had to stay away from the Christ business. Besides, Christ was Shrike's particular joke." As Miss Lonelyhearts leaves the office and walks through a little park, the shadow of a lamppost pierces his side like a spear. Since nothing grows in the park's battered earth, he decides to ask his correspondents to come and water the soil with their tears. He imagines Shrike telling him to teach them to pray each morning, "Give us this day our daily stone," and thinks: "He had given his reader many stones; so many, in fact, that he had only one left—the stone that had formed in his gut."

Jesus Christ, Shrike says, is "the Miss Lonelyhearts of Miss Lonelyhearts." Miss Lonelyhearts has nailed an ivory Christ to the wall of his room with great spikes, but it disappoints him: "Instead of writhing, the Christ remained calmly decorative." Miss Lonelyhearts recalls: "As a boy in his father's church, he had discovered that something stirred in him when he shouted the name of Christ, something secret and enormously powerful." Unfortunately, he recognizes, it is not faith but hysteria: "For him, Christ was the most natural of excitements."

Miss Lonelyhearts tells Betty he is "a humanity lover," but Shrike more aptly identifies him a "leper licker." "If he could only believe in Christ," Miss Lonelyhearts thinks "then everything would be simple and the letters extremely easy to answer." Later he recognizes that "Shrike had accelerated his sickness by teaching him to handle his one escape, Christ, with a thick glove of words." He decides that he has had a part in the general betrayal of suffering mankind: "The thing that made his share in it particularly bad was that he was capable of dreaming the Christ dream. He felt that he had failed at it, not so much because of Shrike's jokes or his own self-doubt, but because of his lack of humility." Miss Lonelyhearts concludes that "with him, even the word Christ was a vanity." When he gets drunk with Doyle, he calls on Christ joyously, and goes home with Doyle to bring the glad tidings to both Doyles, to heal their marriage. He preaches "love" to them and realizes that he is only writing another column, switches to preaching Christ Jesus, "the black fruit that hangs on the crosstree . . . the bidden fruit," and realizes that he is only echoing Shrike's poisoned rhetoric.

What Miss Lonelyhearts eventually achieves, since he cannot believe in the real Christ, and refuses to become a spurious Christ, is Peter's condition. He becomes the rock on which the new church will be founded, but it is the church of catatonic withdrawal. After three days in bed Miss Lonelyhearts attains a state of perfect calm, and the stone in his gut expands until he becomes "an ancient rock, smooth with experience." The Shrikes come to take him to a party at their apartment, and against this rock the waves of Shrike dash in vain. When Mary wriggles on Miss Lonelyhearts' lap in the cab, "the rock remained perfect." At the party he withstands Shrike's newest mockery, the Miss Lonelyhearts Game, with indifference: "What goes on in the sea is of no interest to the rock." Miss Lonelyhearts leaves the party with Betty: "She too should see the rock he had become." He shamelessly promises her marriage and domesticity: "The rock was a solidification of his feeling, his conscience, his sense of reality, his self-knowledge." He then goes back to his sickbed content: "The rock had been thoroughly tested and had been found perfect."

The next day Miss Lonelyhearts is burning with fever, and "the rock became a furnace." The room fills with grace, the illusory grace of madness, and as Doyle comes up the stairs with a pistol Miss Lonelyhearts rushes downstairs to embrace him and heal his crippled leg, a miracle that will embody his succoring all suffering mankind with love. Unable to escape Miss Lonelyhearts' mad embrace, terrified by Betty coming up the stairs, Doyle tries to toss away the gun, and Miss Lonelyhearts is accidentally shot. He falls dragging Doyle down the stairs in his arms.

It is of course a homosexual tableau—the men locked in embrace while the woman stands helplessly by—and behind his other miseries Miss Lonelyhearts has a powerful latent homosexuality. It is this that is ultimately the joke of his name and the book's title. It explains his acceptance of teasing dates with Mary and his coldness with Mary; he thinks of her excitement and notes: "No similar change ever took place in his own body, however. Like a dead man, only friction could make him warm or violence make him mobile." It explains his discontent with Betty. Most of all it explains his joy at being seduced by Fay—"He had always been the pursuer, but now found a strange pleasure in having the roles reversed"—and how quickly the pleasure turns to disgust.

The communion Miss Lonelyhearts achieves with Doyle in Delehanty's consists in their sitting silently holding hands, Miss Lonelyhearts pressing "with all the love he could manage" to overcome the revulsion he feels at Doyle's touch. Back at the Doyles, after Doyle has ripped open Miss Lonelyhearts' fly and been kicked by his wife, they hold hands again, and when Fay comes back in the room she says "What a sweet pair of fairies you guys are." It is West's ultimate irony that the symbolic embrace they manage at the end is one penetrating the body of the other with a bullet.

We could, if we so chose, write Miss Lonelyhearts' case history before the novel begins. Terrified of his stern religious father, identifying with his soft loving mother, the boy renounces his phallicism out of castration anxiety—a classic Oedipus complex. In these terms the Shrikes are Miss Lonelyhearts' Oedipal parents, abstracted as the father's loud voice and the mother's tantalizing breast. The scene at the end of Miss Lonehearts' date with Mary Shrike is horrifying and superb. Standing outside her apartment door, suddenly overcome with passion, he strips her naked under her fur coat while she keeps talking mindlessly of her mother's death, mumbling and repeating herself, so that Shrike will not hear their sudden silence and come out. Finally Mary agrees to let Miss Lonelyhearts in if Shrike is not home, goes inside, and soon Shrike peers out the door, wearing only the top of his pajamas. It is the child's Oedipal vision perfectly dramatized: he can clutch at his mother's body but loses her each time to his more potent rival.

It should be noted that if this is the pattern of Miss Lonelyhearts' Oedipus complex, it is not that of West, nor are the Shrikes the pattern of West's parents. How conscious was West of all or any of this? I would guess, from the book's title, that he was entirely conscious of at least Miss Lonelyhearts' latent homosexuality. As for the Oedipus complex, all one can do is note West's remarks in "Some Notes on Miss Lonelyhearts": "Psychology has nothing to do with reality nor should it be used as motivation. The novelist is no longer a psychologist. Psychology can become much more important. The great body of case histories can be used in the way the ancient writers use their myths. Freud is your Bulfinch; you can not learn from him."

The techniques West uses to express his themes are perfectly suited to them. The most important is a pervasive desperate and savage tone, not only in the imagery of violence and suffering, but everywhere. It is the tone of a world where unreason is triumphant. Telling Miss Lonelyhearts that he is awaiting a girl "of great intelligence," Shrike "illustrated the word *intelligence* by carving two enormous breasts in the air with his hands." When Miss Lonelyhearts is in the country with Betty, a gas station attendant tells him amiably that "it wasn't the hunters who drove out the deer, but the yids." When Miss Lonelyhearts accidentally collides with a man in Delehanty's and turns to apologize, he is punched in the mouth.

The flowering cactus that blooms in this wasteland is Shrike's rhetoric. The book begins with a mock prayer he has composed for Miss Lonelyhearts, and every time Shrike appears he makes a masterly speech: on religion, on escapes, on the gospel of Miss Lonelyhearts according to Shrike. He composes a mock letter to God, in which Miss Lonelyhearts confesses shyly: "I read your column and like it very much." He is a cruel and relentless punster and wit. In his sadistic game at the party, Shrike reads aloud letters to Miss Lonelyhearts. He reads one from a pathetic old woman who sells pencils for a living, and concludes: "She has rheum in her eyes. Have you room in your heart for her?" He reads another, from the paralyzed boy who wants to play the violin, and concludes: "How pathetic! However, one can learn much from this parable. Label the boy Labor, the violin Capital, and so on . . ." Shrike's masterpiece, the brilliant evocation of the ultimate inadequacy of such escapes as the soil, the South Seas, Hedonism, and art, is a classic of modern rhetoric, as is his shorter speech on religion. Here are a few sentences from the latter: "Under the skin of man is a wondrous jungle where veins like lush tropical growths hang along overripe organs and weed-like entrails writhe in squirming tangles of red and yellow. In this jungle, flitting from rock-gray lungs to golden intestines, from liver to lights and back to liver again, lives a bird called the soul. The Catholic hunts this bird with bread and wine, the Hebrew with a golden ruler, the Protestant on leaden feet with leaden words, the Buddhist with gestures, the Negro with blood."

The other cactus that flowers in the wasteland is sadistic violence. The book's most harrowing chapter, "Miss Lonelyhearts and the Lamb," is a dream or recollection of a college escapade, in which Miss Lonelyhearts and two other boys, after drinking all night, buy a lamb to bar' ecue in the woods. Miss Lonelyhearts persuades his companions to sacrifice it to God before barbecuing it. They lay the lamb on a flower-covered altar and Miss Lonelyhearts tries to cut his throat, but succeeds only in maiming it and breaking the knife. The lamb escapes and crawls off into the underbrush, and the boys flee. Later Miss Lonelyhearts goes back and crushes the lamb's head with a stone. This nightmarish scene, with its unholy suggestions of the sacrifices of Isaac and Christ, embodies the book's bitter paradox: that sadism is the perversion of love.

Visiting Betty early in the novel, aware "that only

violence could make him supple," Miss Lonelyhearts reaches inside her robe and tugs at her nipple
unpleasantly. "Let me pluck this rose," he says, "I
want to wear it in my buttonhole." In "Miss Lonelyhearts and the Clean Old Man," he and a drunken
friend find an old gentleman in a washroom, drag
him to a speakeasy, and torment him with questions
about his "homosexualistic tendencies." As they get
nastier and nastier, Miss Lonelyhearts feels "as he
had felt years before, when he had accidentally
stepped on a small frog. Its spilled guts had filled
him with pity, but when its suffering had become
real to his senses, his pity had turned to rage and he
had beaten it frantically until it was dead." He ends
by twisting the old man's arm until the old man
screams and someone hits Miss Lonelyhearts with a
chair.

The book's only interval of decency, beauty, and
peace is the pastoral idyll of the few days Miss
Lonelyhearts spends with Betty in the country. They
drive in a borrowed car to the deserted farmhouse
in Connecticut where she was born. It is spring, and
Miss Lonelyhearts "had to admit, even to himself,
that the pale new leaves, shaped and colored like
candle flames, were beautiful and that the air smelt
clean and alive." They work at cleaning up the
place, Betty cooks simple meals, and they go down
to the pond to watch the deer. After they eat an
apple that has ominous Biblical overtones, Betty re-
veals that she is a virgin and they go fraternally to
bed. The next day they go for a naked swim; then,
with "no wind to disturb the pull of the earth,"
Betty is ceremonially deflowered on the new grass.

The reader is repeatedly warned that natural innocence cannot save Miss Lonelyhearts: the noise of birds and crickets is "a horrible racket" in his ears; in the woods, "in the deep shade there was nothing but death—rotten leaves, gray and white fungi, and over everything a funereal hush." When they get back to New York, "Miss Lonelyhearts knew that Betty had failed to cure him and that he had been right when he had said that he could never forget the letters." Later when Miss Lonelyhearts is a rock and leaves Shrike's party with Betty, he tries to create a miniature idyll of innocence by taking her out for a strawberry soda, but it fails. Pregnant by him and intending to have an abortion, Betty remains nevertheless in Edenic innocence; Miss Lonelyhearts is irretrievably fallen, and there is no savior who can redeem.

The book's pace is frantic and its imagery is garish, ugly, and compelling. The letters to Miss Lonelyhearts are "stamped from the dough of suffering with a heart-shaped cookie knife." The sky looks "as if it had been rubbed with a soiled eraser." A bloodshot eye in the peephole of Delehanty's glows "like a ruby in an antique iron ring." Finishing his sermon to the "intelligent" girl, Shrike "buried his triangular face like the blade of a hatchet in her neck." Miss Lonelyhearts' tongue is "a fat thumb," his heart "a congealed lump of icy fat," and his only feeling "icy fatness." Goldsmith, a colleague at the paper, has cheeks "like twin rolls of smooth pink toilet paper." Only the imagery of the Connecticut interlude temporarily thaws the iciness and erases the unpleasant associations with fatness and thumb. As Miss Lonelyhearts watches Betty naked, "She looked a little fat, but when she lifted something to the line, all the fat disappeared. Her raised arms pulled her breasts up until they were like pink-tipped thumbs."

The unique greatness of *Miss Lonelyhearts* seems to have come into the world with hardly a predecessor, but it has itself influenced a great many American novelists since. *Miss Lonelyhearts* seems to me one of the three finest American novels of our century. The other two are F. Scott Fitzgerald's *The Great Gatsby* and Ernest Hemingway's *The Sun Also Rises*. It shares with them a lost and victimized hero, a bitter sense of our civilization's falsity, a pervasive melancholy atmosphere of failure and defeat. If the tone of *Miss Lonelyhearts* is more strident, its images more garish, its pace more rapid and hysterical, it is as fitting an epitome of the thirties as they are of the twenties. If nothing in the forties and fifties has similarly gone beyond *Miss Lonelyhearts* in violence and shock, it may be because it stands at the end of the line.

STANLEY EDGAR HYMAN